You're invited to a

CREEPOVER™

Truth or Dare...

written by P. J. Night

SIMON SPOTLIGHT

Spotlight

visit us at www.abdopublishing.com

Reinforced library bound edition published in 2013 by Spotlight, a division of the
ABDO Group, PO Box 398166, Minneapolis, MN 55439. Spotlight produces
high-quality reinforced library bound editions for schools and libraries.
Published by agreement with SIMON SPOTLIGHT.

Printed in the United States of America, North Mankato, Minnesota.

102012

112013

This book contains at least 10% recycled materials.

SIMON SPOTLIGHT
An imprint of Simon & Schuster Children's Publishing Division

Library of Congress Cataloging-in-Publication Data

This book was previously cataloged with the following information:

Night, P.J.
Truth or dare-- / written by P.J. Night.
    p. cm. -- (You're invited to a creepover)
When Abby Miller confesses her crush on Jake during a game of Truth or Dare and
then receives a text message warning her to stay away from him, she starts suspecting
that her stalker is a ghost, and not a jealous classmate.
[1. Ghosts—Fiction. 2. Interpersonal relations—Fiction. 3. Schools—Fiction.] I. Title.
PZ7.N576 Tr 2011
[Fic]

2010048170

ISBN 978-1-61479-065-5 (reinforced library bound edition)

All Spotlight books are reinforced library bindings
and manufactured in the United States of America.

PROLOGUE

Up and down the aisles she wandered, and though so much was familiar, there were small and unexpected differences: The lights seemed brighter, the colors looked bolder, even the sounds were louder. She smiled a little, to think how fascinated she was by a grocery store. How many times had she been in one before and hardly noticed a thing about it? Felt bored, even?

Now that seemed like a long time ago.

And here she was, drinking it all in, appreciating it, even appreciating the people around her, who weren't paying her any attention as they hurried past one another, obviously preoccupied.

Then she saw them, two girls around her age, one tall with long, straight chestnut hair; the other a little shorter, her blond hair pulled back from her face. She watched how they giggled together, how the taller one leaned down to whisper something, a secret that they shared, their heads nearly touching. She wished she knew what they were talking about. It wasn't hard to tell that they were best friends; and a pang of longing made her want to look away. But she didn't. Instead she stared harder.

Did they have any idea how lucky they were?

CHAPTER 1

Abby Miller stared at the contents of the grocery cart. "Okay, we've got soda, we've got veggies and dip, we've got popcorn," she said. "Do we need anything else?"

"What about chips?" Leah Rosen, Abby's best friend, asked.

Abby nodded. "You go get some chips and I'll find something good for breakfast."

Leah disappeared around the corner, leaving the cart behind for Abby. Abby wandered through the store to the frozen food section and stood in front of the breakfast case, weighing the waffle options: plain or buttermilk or blueberry or apple cinnamon or—

Suddenly Abby had the creepiest feeling that she was being watched. In the chrome edges of the case, she thought she saw something move.

But when she glanced behind her, no one was there.

She was the only person in the frozen food aisle.

Abby turned back to the freezer case and opened the glass door. She was reaching for a box of buttermilk waffles when—

"BOO!"

Abby shrieked as she felt a swift tug on her hair. She spun around to see Leah grinning at her.

"Gotcha!" Leah exclaimed. "Wow, I really spooked you, huh? You have goose bumps!"

"Yeah, from the freezer." Abby laughed, gesturing to the frosty air pouring out of the open case.

"Sure, Ab. Whatever you say," Leah replied, her eyes twinkling. "Check out what I got!"

Abby wrinkled her nose. "Barbecue chips? You know I don't like barbecue!"

"More for me," Leah said with a grin. "Don't worry, you're covered." She tossed a bag of tortilla chips into the cart and placed a jar of salsa next to it.

Abby added two boxes of frozen waffles. "We'll order the pizzas after everybody else gets to my house, so I think that's about everything we need."

Leah frowned. "You're forgetting one essential—dessert!"

"What's wrong with me?" Abby said, laughing. "What should we get? Cookies?"

"Brownies?" suggested Leah. The girls exchanged a glance.

"Both!" they said at the same time.

"Come on, desserts are in the next aisle," Leah said as she pushed the cart around the corner. Suddenly she backed up—right into Abby!

"Leah! What are you—," Abby began.

But Leah frantically waved her hands at her friend and whispered, "Shh! Shh!"

"What? What is it?" Abby asked as she followed Leah to the opposite end of the aisle.

Leah leaned close to Abby's ear and whispered, "Max! Max Menendez! He's right over there getting candy! Do I look okay?"

Abby reached out and smoothed out the bumps in her friend's blond ponytail. It was no secret that Leah had a major crush on Max. Every time she was around him, she got so nervous that she could barely speak. "You look great," Abby assured Leah. "Want to go say hi?"

"Are you crazy?" Leah gasped as she tried to get a

glimpse of her reflection in the freezer case's shiny silver handle.

"Come on!" Abby urged her friend as she gave Leah a little push. "This is a perfect opportunity to talk to him! I'll come with you."

But Leah shook her head. "I'll probably say something stupid," she replied. "Let's just wait here until he leaves."

"Come on, Leah!" Abby whispered. "How will you two ever go out if you won't talk to him? And this'll be a great story to tell Chloe and Nora at the party tonight."

"Party? What party?" a voice asked.

Leah and Abby spun around.

It was Max!

He smiled at the girls. "You're having a party and you didn't invite me?"

Abby looked at Leah, thinking it would be the perfect time for her friend to say *something* to Max. But Leah just stood there—as frozen as the peas across the aisle. Her eyes were so wide that she even looked a little scared.

"Um . . . of course we didn't invite you," Abby said, grinning playfully as she tried to save the situation. "It's a sleepover party. No boys allowed."

"Well, *fine*," Max said, pretending to be hurt. "I'm busy, anyway."

"Oh yeah?" asked Abby. "Doing what?"

"Wouldn't you like to know?" Max said with a laugh. "Nah, I'm just messing with you guys. I'm going to a movie with Jake and Toby. I thought I'd snag some candy before the show."

"That's cool," Abby said as her eyes lit up. She didn't notice the way Leah began to watch her. "What are you guys gonna see?"

"Don't know yet," Max replied. He laughed. "I mean, obviously some snacks were the priority, you know?"

"Well, have fun," Abby said. "We've gotta go. See you later, Max."

"See you guys," Max said. "Hey, Leah—heads up!"

Leah jumped as Max tossed a candy bar to her. "I got too much," he said with a smile. "You want one?"

"Uh, yeah, sure," Leah stammered. "Th-thanks, Max."

Max flashed another grin at the girls as he sauntered down the aisle. As soon as he was gone, Leah grabbed Abby's arm. "*Wow! He* gave *me* a candy bar!"

Abby smiled at Leah's excitement. "Kind of," she pointed out. "You still have to pay for it."

But Leah was too distracted to pay attention to Abby. "Max is so cute!" she gushed. "I wish I didn't get so tongue-tied around him."

"Just relax," Abby said to her friend. "He's only a boy."

"Only a boy!" exclaimed Leah. "How are you not as in love with him as I am?"

Abby thought for a moment about Max's spiky black hair and his big smile. He was definitely a hottie—but there was a guy at school who Abby thought was even hotter. "Yeah, he's pretty awesome," she said carefully.

But Leah gave Abby a piercing look. "You think there's somebody cuter than Max?" she asked. "Who?"

Abby pressed her lips together and shook her head. Her crush was top secret—and she wanted to keep it that way.

"Oh, come on, Abby," Leah begged. "I told you a million years ago that I liked Max. You owe me!"

Abby laughed. "I'm not telling. It's not my fault you can't keep your own secrets."

"I'll figure out who it is," Leah said. "It's not Toby, is it?"

"Not even close," Abby replied. "Now would you please stop? I'm not telling!"

Leah clapped her hands. "I know! I know! It's Jake, isn't it?"

Abby's mouth dropped open. "No! Why would you even think that?"

"*Jake?*" squealed Leah. "Seriously? You like *Jake?*"

"No way," Abby said firmly. "Please, can you drop it? I mean it, Leah."

Leah sighed. "Fine, be that way. But I *will* find out for sure who you like."

Abby was silent as she pushed the cart toward the produce aisle to get some strawberries for breakfast. She knew that when Leah was determined to find something out, there was no stopping her.

And Abby also knew that even though Leah was her very best friend, she couldn't keep a secret. Leah might be shy around boys, but she wasn't shy when it came to gossip. Abby knew she meant well, but telling Leah something in confidence was as good as posting it online.

Before long, the whole world would know it too.

After Abby and Leah finished buying everything they needed for the sleepover, Abby's mom drove them to Abby's house. They had just started unloading the groceries when there was a loud knock at the door. Chester, the Millers' oatmeal-colored cocker spaniel, jumped up and ran toward the door, yipping in excitement.

"Woo-hoo!" Abby exclaimed as she hurried out of the kitchen. She flung open the front door to find her friend Nora Lewis waiting there, holding a purple duffel bag, a pink sleeping bag, and a stack of DVDs.

"Am I too early?" Nora asked as she walked inside. "My brother had to drop me off before he went to work."

"No, you're fine," said Abby. "Leah and I were just getting some snacks ready."

"Hey, Nora," Leah said, pouring the tortilla chips into a bowl. "Which movies did you bring?"

Nora's brown eyes lit up. "I raided my brother's DVD stash!" she said excitedly as she spread three DVD cases across the counter. "What do you think?"

Abby grabbed one of the cases and read the title. "*Attack of the Bee People?*" she asked.

"Oh, it's *sooo* funny," Nora said. "It's this movie from forever ago, and it was supposed to be really scary, but the special effects are horrible! It's hilarious!"

"What's this one?" asked Leah curiously. "*A Love Beyond?* Seriously?"

Nora sighed. "*Very* romantic. This guy dies, but he

never stops loving this girl, even though she tries to go on with her life. My brother would kill me if it got out that he owned this."

Abby picked up the last DVD case, which had a black cover with a pair of spooky green eyes on it. "*The Hole*," she said as she read the title aloud. "This one looks scary."

"It is," Nora said, nodding. "It's about a cursed grave that can never be closed, and whenever anybody visits the person who was buried there, they get sucked into it too."

"Cool!" Leah exclaimed. "I love scary movies! Let's save that one for right before we go to sleep."

Abby shook her head as she dropped the DVD back on the counter. "No way," she said firmly. "If we watch that one last, I'll be way too scared to sleep."

Leah laughed. "Exactly! Then we'll stay up all night for sure!"

There was another knock at the door.

"Got it," Abby said as she darted into the hallway. When she opened the front door, she found her friend Chloe Chang waiting on the front porch. Chester barked in greeting.

"Hi, Abby!" said Chloe as she stepped inside. "Hi, Chester."

"I'm so glad you're here!" Abby exclaimed. "Leah and Nora are in the kitchen."

"Excellent," Chloe said as she gave Chester a pat on the head and followed Abby into the house. "I've been looking forward to this sleepover all day!"

"Hey!" Leah said as she waved to Chloe. "Abby, did you unpack the cookies and brownies? I can't find them."

Abby shook her head. "Maybe we left a bag in the car," she replied. "I'll go check." She grabbed her mom's car keys and hurried outside.

Abby's brown hair fluttered in the cool, damp breeze; in the distance, dark clouds threatened to bring a rainstorm before morning. She unlocked the car and found one last grocery bag that had fallen under the backseat.

Then Abby felt it again: that spooky sense that someone was watching her, just as she'd felt in the grocery store.

In the silence, she heard a crackling sound, like the crunch of fallen leaves. Almost like footsteps.

But that's not possible, she thought. Abby's house was located at the end of a suburban street, next to a woodland nature preserve where people were forbidden to trespass. In all the years she'd lived there, Abby had never seen anyone in the woods.

She'd never stepped foot in them either, not with all the large NO TRESPASSING signs, bright orange warnings that were impossible to miss.

But as she stood in the driveway, Abby couldn't shake the feeling that someone was standing just beyond the trees, watching her.

Then she heard another sound coming from the woods. This one was familiar, but she couldn't place it. It was sort of like the rusty squeak of an old swing set on a stormy day, when the wind pushes the swings like invisible hands.

But there weren't any swing sets here.

Abby took a deep breath and spun around. "Hello?" she called loudly. "Who's there?"

The noise suddenly stopped. The silence was over-whelming.

Someone heard me, she thought.

"Hello?" she called again. A few moments passed. As she glanced at the nature preserve, Abby started to feel silly. *Are you some kind of baby?* she scolded herself. *Why are you getting all freaked out for absolutely no reason?*

Suddenly a creature burst out of the trees. The black blur took to the sky, cawing noisily, beating its wings with tremendous power as it flew away from the forest as fast as it could.

A crow, Abby thought with relief; she almost laughed out loud. *It was just a crow.* She grabbed the grocery bag and slammed the car door shut. She turned toward the house. She was eager to get inside and forget about the fear that had spread through her whole body as she stood, all alone, by the car.

The first thing Abby saw when she opened her door was Chester standing by the front window, growling quietly. She wanted to believe he was growling at the squirrels in the yard, but she couldn't help but think that the same thing that had spooked her had also spooked her dog. No matter how hard she tried, Abby couldn't stop thinking about the strange squeaking sound coming from somewhere in the woods, just beyond the trees.

And she couldn't shake the feeling that someone— or something—had been watching her.

CHAPTER 2

The kitchen was bright and cheery when Abby returned with the missing grocery bag. She grinned at her friends as she joined them at the table, where they'd already started digging into the snacks. Abby had decided not to tell anybody about what had happened out by the car. But she kept glancing out the window at the woods.

"How many pizzas should I get?" Leah called as she held the cell phone up to her ear. "Two? Three? The phone is ringing and—Hello? I'd like to place an order for delivery."

"Two pizzas," Abby said. "One plain and one pepperoni?"

"Sounds good to me," Chloe said as Nora nodded.

"Hey, check this out," Chloe continued as she dug

around in her backpack. "Guess what I brought?"

"Your teddy bear?" teased Abby.

"Ha, ha," Chloe said sarcastically. "A makeover kit! It has every color lipstick you can imagine and a hundred shades of eye shadow."

Nora smiled. "Score!"

"Okay, the pizzas will be here in thirty minutes or less," Leah said as she ended her call. "What should we do until then?"

"Let's go down to the basement," Abby suggested. "We can move the furniture and set up the sleeping bags and stuff, and by the time we're done the pizzas should be here."

She grabbed the DVDs off the counter and followed her friends down the stairs. The awesome sleepover she'd been planning all week was about to begin.

And Abby couldn't wait!

After they were completely stuffed with pizza, the girls returned to the basement. It was one of Abby's favorite rooms in the house. It was set into a gentle hillside so that only part of it was underground; the other half of the basement had large windows that opened onto the backyard and the nature preserve on the side of the house. There was an overstuffed L-shaped couch covered with lots of squishy throw pillows. It was the favorite spot of her mom's black cat, Eddie, who spent most of his time in the basement avoiding Chester. Across from the couch, a large flat-screen TV was mounted on the wall. The rest of the walls were covered in cool vintage movie posters that Abby's parents had collected over the years. When all the colorful sleeping bags were spread out on the floor and the side table was covered with platters of yummy snacks, the basement turned into the perfect place for a sleepover party.

"Makeover time!" Chloe announced as she placed a pink case on the table in the middle of the room. The other girls crowded around as Chloe flipped open the lid to reveal three levels of trays, each one cluttered with a rainbow of cosmetics. The bottom of the case had a large drawer jammed with dozens of hair accessories.

"Is that *blue* mascara?" Leah asked, grabbing a tube. "I have to try that."

"Anyone want to give me a manicure?" asked Chloe. "My nails are a mess."

17

"Sure," Nora replied as she reached for a nail file. "What color do you want?"

Chloe frowned. "Purple?" she asked as she considered her choices. "Or pink? Or maybe silver?"

"Nora, can I do your hair?" Abby asked. "It's so gorgeous."

Nora shrugged. "Sure. But good luck. These curls do their own thing."

Leah stared into the mirror. "What do you guys think? Too much?"

Abby tried not to laugh as she glanced at Leah's crazy-heavy eye makeup; in addition to the blue mascara, she'd added purple eyeliner and two shades of glitter eye shadow. "Well, it depends what look you're going for," she began. "Cute girl on a Saturday night? Yeah, a little much. Going back in time to a disco in the seventies? Then you look perfect!"

Leah reached for the bottle of makeup remover. "I always go overboard with the eye shadow." She sighed.

"Just remember, less is more," Nora advised.

"Except when it comes to your hair, Nora," Abby said as she struggled with a round brush.

Nora laughed. "Hey, don't say I didn't warn you!"

An hour later the girls were just about done with their makeovers. Abby had never seen so many wild eye-shadow pairings and outrageous hairstyles. At least, not since her last sleepover.

"You know what? I think it's time for a little Truth or Dare," Leah suggested slyly, twirling one of her high pigtails around her finger.

"Ooh, yes!" squealed Chloe. "I *love* Truth or Dare!"

"I'm game," said Abby. "How about the person with the craziest hairdo has to go first?"

Chloe started laughing uncontrollably. "Then no doubt you're up, Nora."

"This mess on my head is all Abby's fault," replied Nora, "but sure, I'll go."

"All right, then, Nora," Chloe began, her eyes twinkling. "Truth or dare?"

Nora bit her lip as she thought about her options. "Dare," she said. "What have I got to lose now?"

"Great. I have a good one." Chloe grinned at her. "I dare you to go into the front yard and pretend you're a chicken. And I mean squawking and bawking and everything. For one whole minute."

Abby frowned slightly, remembering the spooky

19

feeling she'd had when she grabbed the grocery bag from the car earlier in the evening. "We don't have to go outside," she said quickly. "Nora can just do the dare down here."

"But it's way more embarrassing if she does it outside," Chloe pointed out. "I mean, somebody could *see* her!"

"No kidding," Abby said. "Did you forget that Jake Chilson lives right across the street?"

"But Jake's at the movies with Max and Toby," Leah reminded her. "And it's Chloe's dare. She gets to set the rules—no matter how heartless they are."

As everyone laughed, Nora rolled her eyes. "Whatever. It's dark. No one will see me." She held her head confidently as she climbed up the basement stairs, with everyone following behind her. When the girls walked outside, Abby saw that Nora was right about how dark it was. The moon was hidden behind some storm clouds; it was so pitch-black that she could barely see her own yard.

Or the trees looming at the edge of the nature preserve.

"Don't start yet," Chloe said. She turned to Abby.

"Do you guys have any lights in the front yard?"

"Yeah, I'll go turn them on." Abby ran over to the side of the house and flipped the big utility switch. Suddenly the front yard was flooded with light that spilled into the street, all the way over to Jake's yard. Abby snuck a glance at the sprawling red house; even though the curtains were drawn, she could tell that the lights were on in the living room. She had lived across the street from Jake for her entire life; in fact, one of her earliest memories was of the two of them digging around in the sandbox in his backyard. They had played together a lot when they were younger, but Abby hadn't been over to his house since the fifth grade. She wondered briefly if Jake still had the same spaceship wallpaper in his room, and smiled to herself as she rejoined her friends in the front yard.

"Oh, man," groaned Nora. "Abby! I didn't know your house had, like, floodlights!"

"That's not all!" Chloe announced as she whipped out her cell phone. "Smile for the camera, Nora!"

"What!" Nora cried. "You're going to *film* me?"

"Absolutely," Chloe said wickedly, holding the cell phone up so the camera would catch all of Nora's chicken impression. "Don't worry, you look fabulous!"

Nora frowned. "No fair!"

"I never said that I *wasn't* going to film you," Chloe protested. "But I guess I can skip it, Nora. If you're feeling *chicken*, I mean."

Nora gave her friend a look. "Ha, ha. Very funny, Chloe. Let me just start so I can get this over with." She walked onto the grass and began to strut around like a chicken, flapping her arms like wings and clucking, "Bawk, bawk, bawk, bawk!"

Abby and the rest of the girls didn't stop laughing until Chloe stopped filming and said, "Okay, that's one minute. Way to go, Nora. You do an awesome chicken impression."

Even Nora started to laugh as she took a bow. "That was seriously the longest minute of my life!" she complained as the girls traipsed back through the kitchen.

"Here you go, Nora," Abby said as she handed her friend a brownie. "You earned it!"

"Thanks," Nora said with a grin. "Better bring the whole tray downstairs. Truth or Dare isn't over yet!"

As soon as the girls were settled back in the basement, Leah announced, "Okay, since Nora was so brave to make a total fool out of herself—"

"*Bawk, bawk!*" clucked Chloe.

"It's her turn to ask someone," Leah finished. "Go on, Nora."

"All right, I choose our hostess. Truth or dare, Ab?"

Uh-oh, Abby thought as everyone turned to her. *I am definitely not in the mood to act like a chicken!* "Truth," she said firmly.

After all, Abby figured, Truth could never be nearly as embarrassing as the dares her friends could dream up.

Or so she thought.

"All right, Abby," Nora began. "Who do you like?"

Abby's face fell. She noticed Leah sitting across from her, beginning to smile and clearly looking forward to the answer.

"Do I *have* to answer that?" Abby pleaded, already knowing what Nora would say.

"Yes," Nora said matter-of-factly. "You picked Truth, and now you have to answer any question I ask. Those are the rules."

As much as she hated to admit it, Abby knew that Nora was right. "If I tell you . . .," she said slowly. "If I tell you who I like, you have to *promise* not to tell anyone. *Ever.*"

"Oh, we promise," Nora said as she made an X over her heart. "Cross my heart and everything!"

Leah nodded, and Chloe added, "Of *course* we won't tell anybody, Abby. You can trust us!"

"Okay." Abby sighed as her face turned redder. "I . . . like . . ."

No one made a sound as they waited for Abby to confess her crush.

"Jake!" she said at last, covering her face with a pillow.

"I *knew* it!" Leah crowed. "I *knew* you were acting weird in the supermarket earlier!"

"Jake Chilson?" asked Chloe. "Oh, he's supercute!"

"Please don't tell anybody, you guys," Abby begged. "I would die if he found out. Seriously."

"We won't say a word," promised Nora.

"Definitely not," Leah agreed.

There was an awkward pause, and Abby wondered if everyone else was thinking about what had happened last year too.

Suddenly Leah pulled her cell phone out of her pocket.

"What are you doing?" Abby asked suspiciously.

Leah looked up innocently. "I thought I could text Jake and say hi," she said, her eyes wide.

"No!" cried Abby. She lunged for Leah's phone, but Leah was too quick; she jumped out of the way and ran to the other side of the room.

"Please don't text him, Leah," Abby begged.

"Why not?" asked Leah. "I only want to help you like you helped me at the market. Like you said, how will you ever have the chance to go out with Jake if you don't talk to him? I can get the conversation started."

"No!" Abby pleaded. "I *really* don't want you to text Jake!"

"Well, *you* could always text him instead," Nora suggested.

"Oh, no. Absolutely not," replied Abby immediately. "What would I say?"

"Well, you'll never know if you don't try," said Chloe. "Maybe Jake would love it if you texted him."

Abby sighed. She knew her friends were right in a way. It would be great to text Jake if he wanted to text her, too. But what if he didn't want to? Abby decided it was a risk she was willing to take. "Fine! Fine, I'll do it!" she said as she pulled her own phone out of her back pocket. *Jake and I are friends*, Abby thought. *We've known each other forever. It won't be totally weird for me to text him. Probably.*

Abby plunked down on the couch as her friends crowded around her.

"What are you going to write?" Chloe asked excitedly.

Abby shrugged. "I'm not sure," she admitted. "What do you guys think?"

"How about this?" suggested Nora. "Dear Jake, I l-o-o-o-o-ove you. . . ."

Abby frowned playfully and grabbed a pillow and tossed it at Nora.

"Just write, 'Hey,'" Chloe suggested. "Maybe he won't even get the text right now. Maybe his phone will be off."

"Maybe," Abby said. But she didn't sound very hopeful. She sighed again as she typed HEY into her phone. Then she took a deep breath and hit send.

For a few moments, everyone was quiet with anticipation. Then, suddenly, Abby's phone pinged. All the girls shrieked.

"He wrote back! He wrote back!" Abby cried, forgetting her embarrassment as she read Jake's message aloud. "'Hey, Abby! What's up?' Aaaah! What should I write back?" she asked her friends.

"Just say, 'Nothing. What's up with you?'" Chloe advised her.

"That works," Abby replied as she started typing.

Everyone waited anxiously for Jake to reply.

Ping!

When Abby's phone beeped, all the girls screamed in excitement again. This time the cat dashed up the stairs, frightened by the commotion. "Sorry, Eddie," Abby apologized to the cat.

Suddenly the door at the top of the stairs creaked open—and everyone screamed for a third time!

"Girls?" Abby's mother asked. "Is everything okay?"

"Yeah, Mom," Abby said quickly as her friends dissolved into giggles. "Sorry if we're being too loud."

"It's okay, honey," Mrs. Miller replied. "Just try to keep it down after eleven o'clock, okay?"

"Sure," Abby said. "Good night, Mom."

As soon as Mrs. Miller closed the door, Leah reached for Abby's cell. "What did he say?" she asked excitedly.

"Hang on," Abby said, holding the phone away from Leah. She peered at the screen. "He's hanging out with Max and Toby at his house!"

"*What?*" squealed Nora. "Leah said they were all at the movies!"

"I guess they—"

Ping!

Abby read the text to herself, then started laughing so hard she couldn't speak.

"What did he say?" Leah asked, bouncing up and down a little.

Abby glanced up from her phone. "He says they were wondering if Nora is feeling okay!" she cried. "I guess they saw your little chicken dance."

"*Nooooooo!*" groaned Nora. "Chloe, you are so dead! I can't believe you made me do that stupid dare where everybody could see it. And with all those lights on!"

"Sorry," Chloe said with a shrug, but she had such a big smile on her face that the other girls knew she didn't mean it.

Abby didn't say anything as her fingers flew over the keypad.

"What did you write back?" asked Nora.

"I just told him that you felt like dancing." Abby giggled. "You know you've got all the coolest moves!"

"You guys, this is so awful!" Nora moaned. "If they tell everybody at school on Monday, I will die."

Ping!

This time, Abby started laughing before she even finished reading the text. "Jake says they thought Nora was trying to defeat the evil Octopus Girl!" she shrieked. "I think he means you, Leah!"

Leah's hands flew up to her crazy hairdo as everyone turned to look at her. "Eight pigtails!" she groaned. "Oh man, they really *do* look like octopus tentacles!"

Ping!

Ping!

Ping!

Ping!

"What did he say?" Leah asked. "Anything more about any of us?"

Abby held out her phone so everyone could see Jake's latest texts for themselves.

BATTLE OF THE CENTURY

SUPER CHICKEN VS OCTO-GIRL

FOWL MEETS FISH

WHO WILL WIN?

Abby was howling with laughter along with the other girls when a terrible thought struck her. Had Jake and his pals noticed her own wild hairstyle? The double French braids Nora had attempted to give her were so lumpy that they practically looked like stegosaurus spines.

Abby didn't want to know whatever awful nickname

the boys had dreamed up for her. She turned back to her cell phone and sent one more quick text to Jake.

G2G, C U MONDAY! B4N!

Then Abby turned off her phone.

"Abby!" cried Leah. "Why'd you do that? Things were just getting interesting."

"I figured we should quit while we were ahead. You know, before the guys had a chance to nickname the rest of us. Let's watch a movie now," Abby said, trying to change the subject. "*Attack of the Bee People*, anyone?"

"Awesome," Nora said. "I promise you won't be disappointed!"

While Leah set up the DVD, Abby turned off the lights. Then she joined the rest of the girls on the couch. As the movie started, she checked her cell phone to make sure she had turned it off.

Several hours later the basement was dark and quiet. There wasn't a single sound except for the deep, calm breathing of the sleeping girls.

Suddenly the basement was filled with an eerie green glow.

BZZZZZZZZZZZZZZZZZZ!

BZZZZZZZZZZZZZZZZZZ!

BZZZZZZZZZZZZZZZZZZ!

Abby rubbed her eyes as she started to wake up. What *was* that noise? It sounded familiar.

"What's that?" mumbled Leah.

"The bee people!" Chloe gasped, sitting straight up in her sleeping bag.

"No, no, that was just a movie," Abby said sleepily. "I think it's my phone."

BZZZZZZZZZZZZZZZZZZ!

BZZZZZZZZZZZZZZZZZZ!

Abby fumbled around on the floor near her sleeping bag, but she couldn't find her phone anywhere. "Guys, where is my phone?" she asked. "I left it right here when we went to bed."

BZZZZZZZZZZZZZZZZZZ!

BZZZZZZZZZZZZZZZZZZ!

"Abby, is that it?" Nora asked, pointing across the room. Sure enough, Abby's phone was sitting on the table by the stairs, glowing in the darkness. It rattled across the table every time it vibrated.

"Sorry, everybody," Abby apologized as she crawled

out of her sleeping bag. "I swear, I thought I turned it off."

"Who would text you in the middle of the night?" Chloe asked.

"I don't know," Abby said as she picked up her phone. She squinted her eyes as she peered at the message, trying to read what it said.

Her eyes swept across the screen, and before she could stop herself, she gasped in horror.

"Abby! What's wrong?" Leah asked as she stood up. "What does it say?" She grabbed the phone out of Abby's hand as the other girls gathered around, and held it up so that everyone could read the mysterious text message that Abby had received. It said:

LEAVE HIM ALONE. HE'S MINE!!! DON'T MAKE ME TELL YOU TWICE!

CHAPTER 3

"What?" Chloe cried as she grabbed the phone from Leah.

"Somebody get the lights," Nora said nervously.

In the darkness, Leah stumbled over to the stairs and flipped the light switch—but the soft glow from the lamps didn't make the text any less scary. One look at her friends' faces told Abby that they were as terrified as she was.

"Who sent that text?" Abby asked as she reached for her phone, her hands shaking so much that she almost dropped it on the floor. "I don't know this number. Do you guys recognize it?"

One by one, her friends stared at the screen, then shook their heads.

"Did you—did you do anything to upset anybody?" Nora asked, her voice unsure. "Whoever sent this text sounds mad—*really* mad."

"No—I mean, not that I know of," Abby replied, her eyes glued to her phone, reading the creepy text again. "And if I did, I would want somebody to, you know, tell me—not send some freaky message in the middle of the night."

"Why would someone text you at four o'clock in the morning, anyway?" asked Leah.

"And why would they say *that*?" Chloe chimed in. "I mean, who is 'him'?"

No one answered her—but Abby could tell that they were all thinking of Jake. Could it be a coincidence that she'd received this strange message just hours after she had confessed her crush? *I wish I'd kept my mouth shut*, she thought with regret.

Abby wrapped her arms around herself and shivered. "This doesn't make any sense," she said. "What was my phone doing over there on the table? I *always* sleep next to it. And how did it get turned on? I *know* I turned it off before we watched the movie. I don't understand—did one of you—"

"I'm sure nobody messed with your phone," Nora tried to reassure her. "Maybe you just forgot about checking it before bed, and you accidentally left it on the table or something."

Abby shook her head. "No, I don't—"

"You know what?" Leah said suddenly. "Maybe it was a wrong number."

"Maybe," Abby said slowly. "But that still doesn't explain why . . ."

She trailed off, and Leah spoke up. "Listen, here's how I *know* it's a wrong number. Because you're, like, the nicest girl in the world, and nobody who knows you would *ever* send you a message like that." Leah smiled at her friend.

Abby tried to smile back.

"I mean, it's actually really funny, when you think about it," Leah continued. "Since this is obviously a wrong number, whoever sent it thinks she told somebody off—when she really didn't!"

Leah was on a roll. "Oh, I told *her*," she said in a silly high-pitched voice as she imitated the anonymous girl who'd sent the text. "That girl will *definitely* leave my guy alone now!"

There was a brief pause, and then everybody started to giggle.

"You really think it's no big deal?" Abby asked.

"Of course," Leah said confidently. Then she yawned loudly. "Come on, let's go back to sleep. The sun's not even up yet."

Abby turned her phone off and held it for just a moment. Then she put it back on the table by the stairs before returning to her sleeping bag.

For some reason she couldn't quite explain, Abby didn't want to sleep anywhere near it.

The sun was shining brightly when Abby and her friends finally awoke for the day. As the girls ate waffles and strawberries for a late breakfast, Chloe suddenly said, "Maybe it wasn't a wrong number. Maybe it was a prank!"

"Huh?" asked Leah sleepily as she rubbed her eyes.

"That weird text Abby got last night," Nora reminded her. Then she turned to Chloe. "What do you mean?"

Chloe shrugged. "Well, Abby was texting Jake last night, and Jake was hanging out with Max and Toby," she explained. "Maybe one of them thought it would be funny to send her a scary message in the middle of the night. You know those guys. They can act like total idiots sometimes."

"Maybe it was Jake!" Leah exclaimed.

"No," Abby said, shaking her head. "Jake's too nice. He wouldn't do that."

"He might be nice, but he has a wicked sense of humor," Leah said knowingly. "Remember when he and Max convinced Joey Abrams that everybody was going to do the wave in math class, and Joey had to start it since he sat in the first desk? And then Joey jumped up with his arms in the air, but nobody else did?"

"And Ms. Garcia was all, 'Joey? Are you okay?'" remembered Chloe as she cracked up.

"Oh, and remember that time when they broke into Brandon Murphy's locker and covered all his books in sparkly pink wrapping paper? And he had to carry them around like that all day, until he could go home and re-cover them!" added Nora.

The girls laughed at the memory of Brandon shuffling from class to class with his shiny pink book covers grabbing everyone's attention.

"Those pranks were pretty intense. And Joey and

Brandon are some of Jake's best friends!" Leah contin-

ued. "Yeah, I totally wouldn't put it past Jake to prank

you. After all, you *did* text him first last night! And

maybe this is his way of telling you that he likes you."

Abby blushed at the thought that Jake liked her, too,

but she wasn't convinced that it'd been him who texted

her last night.

Chloe recognized the look on her friend's face.

"Don't worry, Abby, I don't think Jake did it. He doesn't

seem like the type of guy who would do something like

that to a girl, you know? I still think it was just a wrong

number."

"Well, there's one way to find out," Leah said. "Why

don't we call the number back and see who picks up?"

"No way," Abby said at once. "Whoever sent that

text was obviously really upset. I don't want to make

them any madder."

"We could ask Jake if he sent the text," suggested

Nora. "Come on, Abby, aren't you curious?"

"Nope," Abby replied, shaking her head. "Not that

curious, anyway. I don't want anyone to know about it.

I'm serious."

Her friends exchanged a glance.

"What would be so bad about that?" asked Nora.

"Because it was weird," Abby said. "Even if it was just a wrong number, even if it was just a prank, it was creepy, and I don't want anyone else to know about it, okay? From now on, consider it a secret. It doesn't leave this house. Just like you swore you wouldn't tell *anyone* that I like Jake. Swear it, okay?"

"Sure," Nora replied, as Chloe nodded in agreement. Then all eyes turned to Leah.

"Leah?" Abby asked.

"Whatever you want, Abby," Leah said loudly. "I swear I won't tell a single, solitary soul!"

"Won't tell what?" asked Mrs. Miller as she walked into the room. "Good morning, girls."

"Oh, I can't tell you, Mrs. Miller," Leah said, widening her eyes innocently. "What happens at Abby's sleepover, *stays* at Abby's sleepover!"

Everyone laughed as Mrs. Miller poured herself a cup of coffee. "Sounds serious," she joked. "I hope you all had fun last night."

"We did," Chloe replied. "Thanks for letting us sleep over."

"Oh, anytime!" Mrs. Miller said.

Just then a car horn honked outside. Chester barked in reply, and Abby peeked out the window. "Hey, Chloe, your mom is here," she said.

"Ack! I still have to pack up my makeover kit!" Chloe cried as she scurried downstairs.

"I'll help you," Nora said, following her.

"So what are you doing today?" Leah asked Abby. "Any awesome plans? Any awesome plans that would be even more awesome with me?"

"Nope," Abby said. "Homework. I have a ton, and I haven't even started yet."

"Boo! You're no fun," Leah said, pouting.

"What about you?" Abby asked. "Did you finish all your homework already?"

"No," admitted Leah. "But that's what Sunday *night* is for—not Sunday *day*."

"Yeah, well, I'll probably still be working tonight," Abby said. "I've barely started my English paper."

"Oh, good, neither have I," Leah said brightly. "I'll text you when I get writer's block!"

There was another honk outside. "That's my mom," said Leah, picking up her plate and putting it in the sink. "Thanks for an awesome sleepover, Abby!

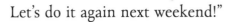

Let's do it again next weekend!"

"Maybe," Abby said with a smile. "I'll talk to you later, okay?"

"You know it," Leah said, grinning over her shoulder at Abby.

After all her friends went home, Abby trudged down the hall to her first-floor bedroom to start her homework. But her bed looked so comfortable that she decided to lie down for just a moment. The next thing she knew, she heard her mother calling her for dinner. *Oh, man*, Abby realized as she blinked her eyes sleepily. *I slept all afternoon! Now I'm going to be up late doing my stupid homework.*

Abby ate dinner as quickly as she could, then hurried back to her desk and logged onto her computer. Just as she opened a new document to start writing her report, an instant message flashed onto her screen. It was from Leah.

Leah601: HEY!!! HOW IS YOUR HOMEWORK GOING? ALMOST DONE?

AbbyGirl: UGH, NO. I FELL ASLEEP AND HAVEN'T EVEN STARTED YET.

Leah601: WELCOME TO MY WORLD.

AbbyGirl: DID U SLEEP ALL AFTERNOON TOO?

Leah601: NO . . . I JUST COULDN'T GET STARTED. I WASN'T IN THE MOOD.

AbbyGirl: WHEN ARE YOU EVER IN THE MOOD FOR HOME-WORK?

Leah601: ☺

Leah601: I JUST COULDN'T STOP THINKING AFTER LAST NIGHT . . .

AbbyGirl: ?

Leah601: I WAS THINKING ABOUT HOW YOU LIKE JAKE.

AbbyGirl: WHAT ABOUT IT?

Leah601: IT MADE ME THINK ABOUT . . .

Abby frowned at the screen. *What's up with Leah?* Then she heard a *ping*; Leah had sent her a link. Abby clicked on it and waited for the website to load. When she saw what was on the website, her heart sank. She knew exactly why her friend had sent her that link. The *ping* of a new message rang through Abby's room.

Leah601: WELL? DID U CHECK IT OUT?

AbbyGirl: YEAH.

Leah601: AND?

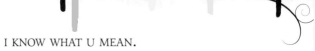

AbbyGirl: I KNOW WHAT U MEAN.

Leah601: IT'S STILL SO SAD.

AbbyGirl: DEFINITELY.

Leah601: ANYWAY, I BETTER GO. HOMEWORK CALLS. SEE YA TOMORROW.

Abby closed the IM window, but she didn't start her report. Instead she found herself clicking back on the website Leah had sent her: the homepage for the Sara James Memorial Scholarship Foundation. As Abby looked at the large picture of Sara on the website, she felt a strong pang of sorrow. She remembered when that picture was taken—almost one year ago, on last year's school picture day. When Sara sat on the metal stool and smiled for the camera, she didn't know that it was the last picture anyone would ever take of her. She didn't know that she had just weeks to live.

Sara and her family had moved to Riverdale two years ago. At a large school like Riverdale Middle, a new student wasn't usually a big deal, but Sara was special. With her long red hair, sparkling green eyes, and mysterious smile, everyone was fascinated by her—especially the boys. It seemed like everybody wanted to

43

get to know her, but Sara was totally into Jake. They had become a couple almost immediately, and Abby hardly ever saw them apart. Abby could still remember them sitting together at a corner lunch table, Jake's head bent low as Sara whispered a secret into his ear, her sleek red hair brushing against his cheek. While most of the other guys in their class were goofing off and acting totally immature, Jake seemed to really be falling in love.

Then everything went terribly wrong one foggy autumn evening as Sara walked home alone after studying at Jake's house. A car rounded the corner just a little too fast, lost control, and swerved onto the sidewalk, slamming into Sara and killing her instantly. Abby remembered all too well the awful days that followed: the small groups of students crying quietly at school; the funeral that was unbearably sad; the scholarship foundation that Sara's grieving parents had started to make sure their beloved daughter would never be forgotten.

And Abby remembered something else, too: the heavy cloud of sadness that seemed to follow Jake everywhere last year. In fact, it was only recently that Jake had started to seem like his old self. It seemed like his summer away at baseball camp had really lifted his spirits. Abby was so happy to see her old friend smiling again. And she started to realize that she liked him as more than just a friend, and maybe he liked her that way too.

But as she looked at the photo of Sara, Abby felt her hope fade. *Even if Jake is ready to go out with someone else, I'm totally not his type. I'm* nothing *like Sara James.*

Suddenly the light on Abby's desk burned out with a loud *pop* that made her jump. In the darkness of the bedroom, the computer monitor gave a spooky glow to Sara's photo on the website. Abby shook her head as she closed the site and went to the basement to find a new lightbulb.

But it was impossible for her to forget those luminous green eyes, gleaming in the darkness.

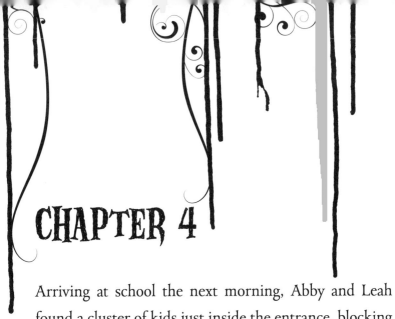

CHAPTER 4

Arriving at school the next morning, Abby and Leah found a cluster of kids just inside the entrance, blocking the front doors. Abby raised her eyebrows as she looked at Leah. "What's going on?" she asked.

"Must be something important," Leah said as she craned her neck, trying to get a glimpse over the crowd. "Or something exciting!"

"Exciting? Here? Yeah, right." Abby laughed as they slowly made their way into the lobby. Just beyond the doors, they saw what all the fuss was about: a large poster announcing the first dance of the school year.

Leah grabbed Abby's arm. "A dance!" she squealed. "I can't wait! And it's the perfect excuse to get a new outfit. What are you going to wear?"

"Let's see," Abby mused. "My gray hoodie and my favorite jeans."

Leah frowned. "You're kidding," she said bluntly. "That is the worst outfit for a dance."

"But it's perfect for lounging around and watching TV," Abby said. "Which is what I will be doing instead of going to some stupid dance."

"Don't be like that," Leah complained. "I know the dances were boring last year, but this is the first dance of this year. That's kind of a big deal."

"Whatever," replied Abby. "Every dance is the same, Leah. They play the same lame music and serve the same nasty cafeteria hot dogs every single time. And all the girls stand around just waiting for *anybody* to ask them to dance while all the guys end up shooting hoops. No thank you. Come on, I need to go to my locker before homeroom."

But Leah hovered near the poster. "Well, here's something different," she said slowly. "It says here that proceeds from the dance will go to the Sara James Memorial Scholarship Fund. You know what that means, right? You-know-who will definitely be there, so—"

"Shhh!" Abby hissed, glancing around to make sure

no one had overhead Leah. "You promised you wouldn't mention that ever again."

"All right, all right," Leah said. "I just want you to come to the dance! It won't be any fun without you. Please?"

"I'll think about it," Abby finally said, just to stop Leah from badgering her.

"That sounds like a yes!" Leah said, clapping her hands. "Now, seriously, what are we going to wear?"

"I'll think about that, too," Abby promised with a laugh. She couldn't stay annoyed with Leah, not after being her best friend since kindergarten—even if it meant suffering through another awful dance in the gym.

But as the days passed, it started to look like Leah was right to be excited. The whole school was buzzing with rumors about the dance, like that the student council's events planning committee had actually hired a DJ and promised to order better food. After school on Wednesday, Abby and Leah joined a group of kids who had gathered around Morgan Matthews, the class president. Morgan was in the process of describing all the improvements she had planned for the dance. "It's the *least* we can do in memory of Sara," she gushed.

Abby resisted the urge to roll her eyes. "Um, I don't think a pizza upgrade is a really special way to remember Sara," she whispered to Leah.

Just then she felt someone tug on her backpack. She turned around to see who was behind her.

It was Jake!

Oh, no, Abby thought in a panic. *Did he overhear me?*

"You know what?" Jake asked in a low voice. "I couldn't agree more."

"Hi, uh, hey, Jake," Abby stammered. "Yeah . . . it's kind of weird, huh?"

"A little bit," Jake said, nodding. "What are you doing now?"

"I was just about to head out for the bus," Abby said.

"It's such a nice day," Jake began. "I was wondering if you'd like to walk home with me."

"Um, yeah," Abby said as her heart started to pound. She shot a quick glance at Leah. "I'll see you later, Leah?"

"I'll call you!" Leah exclaimed as she gave Abby a little wave. "Bye, Abby! Bye, Jake!"

As Abby and Jake crossed the wide school lawn toward the sidewalk, Abby couldn't think of a single thing to say. Finally she blurted out, "So how's your school year going?"

"It's good, so far," Jake replied. "A lot more work this year, huh?"

"Tell me about it," Abby said. "I have *hours* of homework every night."

"Me too!" exclaimed Jake. "I already can't wait for summer vacation."

"Well, that's only eight months away," Abby pointed out.

"Don't remind me," Jake groaned.

Abby smiled at Jake and looked down at her feet. She couldn't remember the last time she'd been so happy to walk home.

"So that dance," Jake began, "it's turning into kind of a big deal, I guess."

"I guess," Abby said carefully. "Everybody seems really excited about it."

"Are you?" Jake asked, shifting his backpack to his other shoulder. "I mean, are you going?"

"Um, yeah," Abby replied. "I think so."

"That's cool," Jake said. "Me too. Do you want a ride?"

"A ride?" repeated Abby.

"Yeah," Jake said. "My mom's going to drive me, so we could give you a ride. If you want one."

"Yeah, sure," Abby said quickly. "That sounds great."

Jake smiled at her, and Abby felt like she had a hundred butterflies fluttering in her stomach. "Great," he repeated. "We'll come over at seven on Saturday."

"Okay," Abby replied. "I'm, um, looking forward to it."

"Me too," Jake said. Then, lowering his voice, he added, "I heard a rumor that there's even going to be *pizza*."

As they rounded the corner of Elmhurst Lane, Abby started to laugh. "Do you mean *really* amazing, *really* delicious pizza?" she asked, imitating Morgan. Jake's laughter told Abby that her impression was spot-on.

"Well, here's my house," Abby said.

"Right," Jake said. "I'll see you around. Later, Abby."

"Bye, Jake," Abby replied as Jake turned to cross the street. She couldn't stop grinning as she walked along the path to her house. When she had almost reached the front door, she dared to glance behind her.

Jake was standing across the street, looking at her—and smiling! When he saw Abby peeking over her shoulder, he held up his hand in a wave. Then he turned away and walked over to his own front door.

Abby opened the door as slowly and calmly as she could, just in case Jake could still see her. But when she got inside, she raced down the hall to her room, smiling so broadly that her cheeks started to ache a little. As she expected, she already had two voice mails, an e-mail, and IMs from Leah.

Leah601: HELLOOOOOO!!

Leah601: WHERE ARE YOU? I AM DYING HERE!!!!!

Abby grinned as she sat down at her computer. She quickly typed a message back to Leah.

AbbyGirl: I'M HERE!!

Leah601: WELL?!?! WHAT HAPPENED?!?!

AbbyGirl: JAKE IS GONNA GIVE ME A RIDE TO THE DANCE!

AbbyGirl: HELLO?

AbbyGirl: DID I LOSE U?

Leah601: SORRY, I FAINTED AND FELL OFF MY CHAIR. R U SERIOUS?! ABBY! U HAVE A DATE W/ JAKE!!!

AbbyGirl: NO, IT'S NOT A DATE, JUST A RIDE :)

Leah601: WHATEVER!! IT'S TOTALLY A DATE. I HATE U SO MUCH. U R SO LUCKY.

AbbyGirl: OH PLZ. IT'S JUST A RIDE.

Leah601: COME ON, HE'S SOOO INTO U! AND U DIDN'T EVEN WANT TO GO TO THE DANCE!

AbbyGirl: LOL, I WANT TO NOW!

Just then Abby heard her mom's voice. "Honey, can you take Chester out?" Mrs. Miller called from the living room. "He won't stop barking, and I'm expecting a phone call any minute now."

"Sure, Mom," Abby called back. Then she typed one more message to Leah.

AbbyGirl: GOTTA TAKE CHESTER FOR A WALK. CALL U LATER?

Leah601: U BETTER! WE HAVE SO MUCH TO DISCUSS! BYE!

Abby bounded down the hall. "Chester!" she said. "Let's go for a walk, cutie!" Chester trotted up to Abby, wagging his tail. She fastened a red leash to the dog's collar and walked toward the front door.

But as they approached the door, Chester's fur

suddenly bristled. His mouth twisted into a snarl as he started growling, a long, low, menacing sound that sent chills up Abby's spine.

"What's the matter, boy?" Abby asked as she moved closer to the door and glanced outside. Across the yard, golden sunlight streamed through the trees in the nature preserve. It looked like a beautiful autumn afternoon—and completely ordinary. Abby couldn't imagine why Chester seemed so tense, but there was definitely something outside that was making him growl so fiercely.

"Shhh, it's okay, Chester," Abby said soothingly as she stroked his head for a few seconds. Eventually he stopped growling, though he wouldn't take his eyes off the door.

But the minute Abby reached for the doorknob, Chester started barking so furiously that Mrs. Miller called out, "Abby! I'm on the phone!"

"Okay, okay!" Abby replied as she scooped up Chester and hurried through the front door. Once they were on the sidewalk in front of the neighbor's lawn, the dog calmed down immediately, but Abby couldn't stop wondering what had bothered him. "Was it a squirrel, buddy?" she asked. "Or another dog, maybe?"

Chester just trotted alongside her, wagging his tail happily. Abby shook her head and gave up trying to figure out what had spooked her pup; she decided to think about more important things as she turned off Elmhurst Lane, like imagining what she and Jake could talk about at the dance. But that made her nervous. She could feel her palms start to sweat. *Why are you being so silly?* she thought. *You've known him forever.* She smiled at her foolishness and started mentally rummaging through her closet instead, analyzing each potential outfit she could wear. *Definitely not a dress*, she mused. *I don't want to look like I'm trying too hard. Maybe my new skirt?*

As dusk began to fall, Chester started to seem a little tired from their long walk. Abby started heading back home. As soon as they got inside, Chester curled up in his dog bed in the living room and fell right asleep.

Abby walked into the kitchen, where her mom was making a big green salad. Eddie was lounging on the kitchen floor, clearly happy that the dog wasn't around. "Mmm, something smells good! What's for dinner?"

"Your favorite—lasagna," her mom said.

Abby's stomach growled. "Score! Can I help?"

Mrs. Miller shook her head. "It's already in the

oven," she explained. "Dinner will be in about half an hour, okay?"

"Yum. I can't wait," Abby said, grabbing a handful of baby carrots from the colander on the counter. Then she paused. "Um, Mom? I have to ask you something."

"Go ahead, honey," Mrs. Miller said as she chopped a tomato.

"Um . . . ," began Abby awkwardly. "There's a dance at school this Saturday night, and, uh . . . Jake Chilson said he could give me a ride—er, his mom would drive, of course—so . . . is that okay?"

Mrs. Miller looked up, smiling at her daughter. "Of course, Abby!" she said. "That's exciting! Is Jake your date?"

"Um, maybe," Abby said, looking down and squirming a little. "It's just a ride to the dance, you know? It's not like a big deal or anything."

"Do you want me to pick you two up when the dance ends?" Mrs. Miller asked.

"Uh, I think Mrs. Chilson will pick us up, but I'll ask Jake," Abby said. "Anyway, I'm going to get started on my homework."

"Okay, sweetie," Mrs. Miller said. "Don't forget to set the table before dinner."

When Abby got back to her computer, she had another instant message waiting from Leah. It said:

Leah601: I FIGURED OUT WHAT U SHOULD WEAR TO THE DANCE, CUZ I'M BRILLIANT! YOUR NEW BLUE TOP (THE ONE WITH THE BELT). IT'S GORGEOUS AND J WILL LOVE IT!

A smile spread across Abby's face. She knew just the top Leah was thinking of; it was pale blue with a skinny black belt that looped around the waist. She pulled the top out of her dresser and tried it on, then examined her reflection in the mirror. The color was a perfect contrast against Abby's dark brown hair. *Leah is brilliant!* she thought happily as she twirled in front of the mirror.

Then, out of the corner of her eye, Abby thought she saw a flash of color in the mirror's reflection. She spun around just in time to catch a glimpse of red outside. She raced over to the window for a better look.

In the twilight, she saw the shadowy figure of a girl running away from the window, right through her yard.

The girl had long red hair.

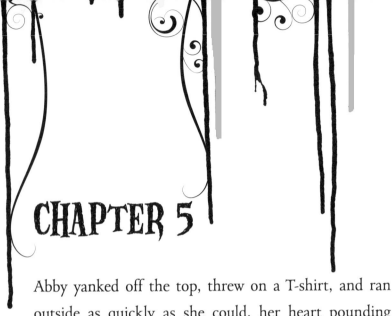

CHAPTER 5

Abby yanked off the top, threw on a T-shirt, and ran outside as quickly as she could, her heart pounding wildly. She was determined to catch up with that girl and find out who she was—and why she was looking in Abby's window.

"Hey!" Abby yelled, careening out the back door. "Who are you? What are you doing here?"

But there was no answer.

She can't be far, Abby thought as she strode through the yard. "I said, *who are you?*" she shouted again.

Still no response.

Abby paused as she reached the edge of the nature preserve. She looked back at her neighbors' yards but didn't see anyone running through them. There was only one possibility: The girl must have disappeared into the woods.

Abby hesitated for just a moment as she glanced at the neon orange sign that read WARNING: TRESPASSERS WILL BE PROSECUTED. She had never set foot in the nature preserve before.

Then again, she'd never caught some stranger staring into her window, either.

Abby took a deep breath and stepped through the wild and overgrown brush. The trees cast long, looming shadows that made Abby shiver—from fear as well as from the sudden chill in the air. The sun was setting. It would soon be dark.

The thought pushed her forward.

"I just want to talk to you," Abby called. "I just want to find out why you were looking in my window."

But the only sound was the crackle of dry, dead leaves being crushed beneath Abby's feet as she walked deeper into the woods. As night seemed to fall faster and faster, she paused. She started to reach for her cell phone.

Suddenly she heard footsteps behind her!

Abby sucked in her breath sharply as she spun around, ready to face whoever had been peeking in her window.

"Hey, kiddo!" Mr. Miller said from the edge of the nature preserve, his suit coat slung over his shoulder. "What are you doing in there? Don't make me call the police to report a trespasser!"

"Ha, ha!" Abby said, so relieved to see her dad that she actually laughed at one of his dumb jokes.

"I thought I saw you run back here when I got home," Mr. Miller continued. "What's going on?"

"Nothing, Dad," Abby said, hoping that her voice sounded normal. With one last glance into the nature preserve, she walked back to her yard. She knew that with her father standing right next to her, there was no hope of finding the mysterious red-haired girl or figuring out why she'd been staring in Abby's window.

"Come on, let's go inside. It's starting to get chilly out," Mr. Miller said. "How was school today?"

"Good," Abby replied. "Mom made lasagna for dinner."

"Fantastic!" exclaimed Mr. Miller as they walked inside. "That sounds delicious."

"Abby, honey, did you set the table?" Mrs. Miller called.

"In a minute, Mom," Abby replied as she reached for

her cell phone, dying to tell Leah all about the strange red-haired girl.

"Abby, it's almost time to eat," Mrs. Miller said as she poked her head out of the kitchen. "Can you please set the table now?"

With a sigh, Abby shoved her phone back into her pocket and walked into the kitchen, where she grabbed a stack of plates and a handful of silverware.

"Did you tell Dad your big news?" asked Mrs. Miller as she carried a platter of sliced bread into the dining room.

"I don't have big news," Abby replied, confused.

"Well, of course you do!" Mrs. Miller exclaimed. "Bob, Jake Chilson asked Abby to go to the dance with him!"

"Mom!" Abby cried. "Why are you making a huge deal out of this?"

"Wait a minute—do I need to have a talk with Jake before you guys head out to the dance?" asked Mr. Miller. He frowned, but Abby could tell by the twinkle in his eyes that he was teasing her.

"Dad, it's just Jake," Abby said. "And he's *just* giving me a ride."

"Still, perhaps I should have a chat with him before—," began Mr. Miller.

"Ugh!" Abby groaned. "Absolutely not! Why are you—"

"Kiddo, I'm just fooling around." Mr. Miller grinned at Abby. "I'm sure you'll have a lot of fun."

Abby sighed once more as she placed the last fork on the table. Then she slipped down the hall to send Leah an instant message in peace.

"Don't get sucked into the Internet, honey," Mrs. Miller called after her. "Dinner is in five minutes!"

"I just have to go hang up my new top, Mom!" Abby replied, rolling her eyes since she knew her mom couldn't see her. "I'll be right back!"

She ducked into her room, closing the door behind her as she breathed a sigh of relief. Then she stopped and sniffed the air, catching a whiff of—what was it? A flowery scent, like jasmine or gardenia, but more exotic. It reminded her of something. Something that she couldn't quite place, a memory that she couldn't quite recall. With a slight frown, Abby sat down at her computer and sent an instant message to Leah.

AbbyGirl: JUST CAUGHT A RED-HAIRED GIRL STARING IN MY WINDOW!!!

Leah601: WHAT???!!!

AbbyGirl: I FOLLOWED HER INTO THE WOODS BUT SHE DISAPPEARED.

AbbyGirl: HER HAIR LOOKED JUST LIKE . . .

Leah601: ???

AbbyGirl: I KNOW IT SOUNDS CRAZY, BUT HER HAIR LOOKED LIKE SARA'S. I'M REALLY WEIRDED OUT.

Leah601: K, SETTLE DOWN. TAKE A DEEP BREATH.

Leah601: EVERYBODY HAS BEEN TALKING ABOUT SARA A LOT, W/ THE DANCE AND ALL . . .

Leah601: AND U PROBABLY FEEL A LITTLE STRANGE FOR GOING ON A DATE W/ JAKE . . .

Leah601: I AM SURE U JUST IMAGINED IT.

Abby's fingers flew over the keyboard as she wrote back.

AbbyGirl: BUT HER HAIR . . . IT LOOKED JUST LIKE SARA'S!!!

Leah responded again in seconds.

Leah601: THAT'S HOW I KNOW U R IMAGINING IT. SARA'S GONE. SO THERE IS NO POSSIBLE WAY THAT THIS REALLY HAPPENED. I PROMISE.

63

Abby paused for a moment as she considered what Leah had written. Was it possible that she had imagined the girl? She had seemed so real, running away from Abby's window. But by the time Abby had reached the backyard, the girl had vanished without a trace.

It would make sense, she realized, if the girl didn't exist at all, if Abby had raced outside to chase a figment of her imagination. After all, it was possible that the red hair Abby thought she saw was just a trick of the light from the setting sun. She felt her cheeks grow warm at the thought.

AbbyGirl: IT SEEMED WAY TOO REAL TO BE MY IMAGINATION.

AbbyGirl: BUT IT'S OVER NOW, I GUESS.

AbbyGirl: DON'T TELL ANYONE, OKAY? I FEEL SOOOOOO STUPID.

Leah601: YOUR SECRET IS SAFE W/ME, SILLY! JUST RELAX AND BE HAPPY.

Leah601: YOUR DREAM GUY ASKED U OUT TODAY! THAT'S SO AWESOME! U SHOULD BE CELEBRATING, NOT FREAKING OUT OVER NOTHING.

AbbyGirl: GOTCHA. LISTEN, I GOTTA GO EAT DINNER. TALK LATER?

Leah601: ABSOLUTELY! I WILL BE HERE.

Abby stood up and pushed in her desk chair. Then she turned around to pick up her top from the floor.

But it wasn't there.

Abby frowned. *I know I tossed it on the floor when I changed to run outside*, she thought, *so where is it?*

She looked in the hamper in the corner of her room, peeked under her bed, and even rummaged through her dresser drawers.

Her beautiful new top was nowhere to be found.

Okay, this is bizarre, Abby thought as she bit her lip. *Where could it be?*

"Abby!" her mom called.

"Be right there!" she yelled back.

Then she glanced at her closet. The door was closed.

A sudden feeling of fear washed over Abby. *I know I didn't close the closet door*, she thought slowly. Step by step, she walked across the room, her heart thudding loudly in her chest. Her hand started to shake as she reached for the smooth brass doorknob; she dreaded opening the door. Who—or what—would she find behind it?

Just do it, she told herself. *One—two—three—*

Abby took a deep breath and yanked open the door. She peered into the dark closet and saw . . .

Her clothes, hanging neatly. Her shoes, arranged in careful pairs on the floor. Her suitcase, tucked in the corner.

Abby was so relieved that she started to laugh out loud. *I can't believe that I was scared to open my own closet door,* she thought. *I have got to chill out.*

Then she saw something blue jammed in the corner of the closet. She reached down to pick it up and realized that she was holding the sleeve of her new top.

Only the sleeve.

The rest of the top, ripped down the middle, was stuffed under her suitcase.

CHAPTER 6

AbbyGirl: U STILL THERE?!?!?!?!

Leah601: YEAH, WHAT'S UP?

AbbyGirl: SOMETHING CRAZY IS DEFINITELY GOING ON! I JUST FOUND MY BRAND-NEW TOP RIPPED UP!

Leah601: HUH?

AbbyGirl: BEFORE I RAN OUTSIDE TO FIND THAT GIRL, I CHANGED OUT OF MY NEW TOP, BUT WHEN I GOT BACK TO MY ROOM, I COULDN'T FIND IT.

AbbyGirl: FINALLY I LOOKED IN MY CLOSET AND MY TOP IS RUINED! IT'S BEEN TORN INTO PIECES! SOMETHING REALLY SCARY IS GOING ON!!!

Leah601: OKAY, OKAY, CALM DOWN. THERE HAS TO BE A REASONABLE EXPLANATION FOR THIS. MAYBE CHESTER GOT IT AND CHEWED IT UP.

AbbyGirl: RIGHT, SO AFTER CHESTER RIPPED UP MY TOP, HE SHOVED IT IN THE BACK OF THE CLOSET AND SHUT THE DOOR?!?!

AbbyGirl: COME ON, HE'S A DOG, THAT DOESN'T MAKE ANY SENSE!!!

Leah601: DON'T YELL @ ME! I'M JUST TRYING TO HELP!

AbbyGirl: SORRY, I'M JUST REALLY FREAKED OUT.

Leah601: MAYBE YOUR MOM CLOSED THE CLOSET DOOR?

AbbyGirl: BUT SHE WOULD HAVE TOLD ME IF SHE CAME IN MY ROOM.

AbbyGirl: AND SHE WOULD HAVE NOTICED IF CHESTER ATE MY SWEATER.

AbbyGirl: AND SHE'S BEEN IN THE KITCHEN THIS WHOLE TIME, COOKING DINNER. IT'S NOT POSSIBLE.

Leah601: THEN I DON'T KNOW WHAT TO TELL U. I MEAN, NO OFFENSE, BUT IT SEEMS LIKE U R TRYING TO FREAK YOUR-SELF OUT.

AbbyGirl: WHAT DO U MEAN?

Leah601: NEVER MIND.

AbbyGirl: NO, SERIOUSLY, TELL ME WHAT U MEAN.

Leah601: JUST FORGET IT.

AbbyGirl: I CAN'T FORGET IT! SOME CRAZY STUFF IS HAPPENING TO ME, AND MY BEST FRIEND IS ACTING LIKE I'M

MAKING IT ALL UP! THX A LOT.

Leah601: WHAT DO U WANT ME TO SAY? THAT SOME STRANGE GIRL WITH RED HAIR MUST BE STALKING U? THAT SARA'S GHOST IS AFTER U?

Leah601: IT'S NOT ENOUGH FOR U THAT THE GUY U LIKE ASKED U TO THE DANCE, NOW U HAVE TO MAKE UP THIS BIG DRAMA SO U CAN BE THE CENTER OF ATTN?

Abby sat back as suddenly as if she'd been slapped in the face. Her eyes darted back and forth as she read Leah's words again. Then, with quivering fingers, she sent another message back to Leah.

AbbyGirl: I DIDN'T KNOW U FELT THAT WAY. I WON'T BOTHER U ANYMORE.

Leah601: ABBY, WAIT. I DIDN'T MEAN IT LIKE THAT. LET'S TALK ABOUT IT, OKAY?

But Abby didn't want to talk to Leah anymore. With a fast click of her mouse, Abby shut the chat window and stepped away from her computer. Just then her cell phone buzzed.

Leah, give it a rest! Abby thought angrily as she picked

69

up her phone. The screen was blinking with a green light to announce that there was a text message waiting for her.

It wasn't from Leah, though. A wrinkle of confusion crossed Abby's forehead as she stared at the phone number. She didn't know whose number it was, but that long combination of digits seemed familiar.

Abby pushed a button so she could read the text. In angry-looking capital letters, the message flashed onto the glowing screen.

I'M WARNING YOU. STAY AWAY FROM HIM!!!! NEXT TIME I WILL DO SOMETHING MUCH WORSE!

As Abby gasped in shock, the phone fell from her fingers; it skidded across the floor until it disappeared under her bed. Another text! After everything that had happened this afternoon, enough was enough. Abby's first instinct was to get to her computer and type the phone number into a search engine to see if she could learn anything about its owner.

She fell into the chair at her desk and tried to type the number into the text box, but her fingers were shaking so much that she kept hitting the wrong keys. She took a deep breath and tried again.

She hit enter.

But the search didn't go through.

With a frown, she hit enter again, but nothing happened. She tried to move the cursor—but her computer was frozen.

"Oh come *on!*" Abby exclaimed as she slammed the keyboard in frustration. She needed to know what was going on *now*. She didn't have time to waste by restarting her computer.

Maybe I can look the number up on my phone, Abby thought as her heart sank. She dreaded seeing that scary message again, but she knew that she had no choice. She dropped to her knees and stuck her head under the bed.

The phone, still glowing, was under the exact middle of Abby's bed. She stretched her arm out to grab it, but the phone was just beyond her reach. With a sigh, she lay down on her stomach and crawled under the bed as far as she could, extending her arm as she reached for the phone.

The minute Abby's fingers curled around her phone, the screen went dark. A freezing blast of air surrounded her; she tried to get out from under the bed but couldn't wiggle free. It was like an unseen hand was holding her down, in the dark, in the cold, and Abby couldn't escape, couldn't move, couldn't breathe.

All she could do was scream!

CHAPTER 7

"ABBY! Abby! What's wrong?" cried Mrs. Miller as she burst into the room, with Mr. Miller and Chester following right behind her.

"Mom!" Abby screamed. "Mom! Help! I can't get out!"

"Honey, honey, calm down," Mrs. Miller said, and Abby felt the warm, comforting touch of her mother's hand on her back. "Let me see. Your T-shirt is caught on the bed frame, honey. Hold on . . . there. You can get out now."

Abby shot out from under the bed, blinking back tears of terror and relief. She wiped her eyes with her hands as she exhaled in a long, jagged sigh. Chester gave her a big lick on the face.

"Kiddo! What's going on? You really scared us," said

Mr. Miller, an expression of concern on his face.

Abby looked at her parents and knew that she needed to tell them everything. "I—I don't know what's happening," she began. "I was trying to look something up online, but then my computer froze, and my whole room got freezing cold and I couldn't get out from under the bed!"

Mr. Miller walked across the room to Abby's computer. "So this old thing's giving you trouble?" he asked. "I can take a look at it after dinner—but you remember how to restart it, right?"

"Dad! That's not the point," Abby exclaimed. "All this weird stuff happened at the same time! I went under the bed and it got *so* cold in here—the air was like ice—"

Mrs. Miller reached out and rested her hand against Abby's forehead. "Are you feeling all right?" she asked. "You don't feel feverish to me."

"You're not listening—," Abby began shrilly as she ducked out from under her mom's hand.

"You know, Abby, this is an old house," Mr. Miller interrupted her as he poked his head under the bed. "There are all sorts of drafts in just about every room. I can see about adding some insulation under the floorboards before winter comes. That would probably help."

"Sweetie, what were you doing under the bed in the first place?" asked Mrs. Miller. She and Mr. Miller exchanged a glance, and in their eyes, Abby saw it: that awful look of parental humoring. They thought she was overreacting, like a small child who was afraid of things that go bump in the night.

That was when Abby realized that there was nothing she could say or do that would convince her parents to take her seriously.

So why even bother?

The text messages, Abby suddenly realized. *I could show them those awful texts.* But then a new thought occurred to her. What if her parents freaked out and took away her phone?

It didn't seem worth the risk.

Abby sighed. "I just . . . I was trying to get my phone. It fell under the bed. It's not important. Forget it."

"Come on, Abby, let's go eat dinner," Mrs. Miller suggested. "I've been calling your name for the last five minutes! Didn't you hear me?"

Abby shook her head as she followed her parents

out of the bedroom. She didn't have much appetite, but she was eager—desperate, even—to get out of her room and away from everything that had just happened there.

Bolstered by a good meal and feeling courageous, Abby hurried back to her bedroom after dinner, but she made sure to leave her door open. If Leah and her parents weren't going to take all these strange things seriously, then Abby would have to figure them out by herself.

Abby's computer hummed to life as she restarted it and logged onto the Internet. For once, she didn't bother checking her e-mail or signing into IM. Instead she opened up Google and searched for the phrase "proof of ghosts."

Dozens of websites flooded the page, promising everything from certified ghost hunters to scary horror movies. But one site in particular caught Abby's eye. She clicked on the link and tapped her fingers impatiently as she waited for the page to load.

When the Paranormal Gets Personal
The only people who can afford not to believe in

ghosts are those who have never been troubled by them. It takes but one encounter with the other world to know that though death waits for us all, the spirit is eternal. Electrical interference, sudden drops in air temperature, unexpected— and unexplained—visions are all calling cards from beyond the grave. Even the most pragmatic disbeliever will find it difficult to explain away all manner of paranormal phenomena, especially when they occur simultaneously.

As she read, Abby started nodding her head. Everything in the article sounded very familiar.

For most spirits, the journey to the other side is an easy one; the gentle letting go of the earthly life is simply part of the natural cycle of being. But some spirits are unprepared for death and find it impossible to tear themselves away from their earthly concerns. This is especially true for those who have suffered untimely death; instead of accepting that their lives were cut short, these spirits long for more—more time with their friends, more time with their families, more time with their loved ones. They are overcome by the sense that they have been cheated of their due; the drive to live becomes like a drug, addictive and intoxicating. With all their strength, these spirits resist the pull of the beyond, desperate to cling to the lives they once lived.

Abby felt a chill run down her spine. She hugged herself tight and glanced at her bedroom door to make sure it was still open . . . just in case.

Sadly for these spirits, there is no going back; once the life force has been extinguished, they find themselves nearly powerless in the earthly realm, unable to be seen or heard (in most cases). This virtual invisibility grows increasingly painful for them, especially as they see their loved ones move through the stages of grief and eventually begin to resume their lives. With a sad and silent farewell, many reluctant spirits will, at this point, resolve to pass over; it is simply too painful for them to watch life from the sidelines.

But some spirits find themselves enraged by these developments, especially if they think that they are being forgotten or replaced. This small number of vengeful spirits should not be confused with those that are simply trying to relay one last, perhaps vital, message to a loved one. Rather, the spiteful spirit will do anything to reclaim his or her former territory, channeling large amounts of electromagnetic energy in an attempt to regain the power of the physical world. Highly charged ions are known to interfere with electronic devices, and clouds of electrons can alter the temperature of the air; scientists have proven this. What modern science has been unable to explain is why sudden, strong pockets of electromagnetism seem to develop out of thin air. Perhaps the air is not as thin as it seems.

With enough practice and motivation, a spirit can summon a quantity of electromagnetism sufficient to scatter paper, knock down books, and create all manner of mischief that generally confuses, befuddles, or frightens the living. There have even been documented reports of "sightings," in which the image of the deceased appears as real as if he or she were still alive. If you have found yourself on the receiving end of such unwanted interference from a restless spirit, be assured that you are not crazy. Read on for suggestions on how to help this misguided spirit find its way to the other realm.

Abby eagerly clicked on the link to read more. What she learned convinced her that she was not imagining things or overreacting. She sat back in her chair, deep in thought. Then she opened up her e-mail and started typing.

To: Leah601
From: AbbyGirl
Subject: Sorry
Hey Leah,
First, I'm sorry I just disappeared like that. I'm really stressing out. So many weird things have been happening and some of them you don't even know about. So I'm going to tell you everything. Please hear me out before assuming it's just my imagination. I wish it was. Because then I could control it and make it STOP.
So right before my party started, I was outside and I had the creepiest feeling that someone was watching me from the woods. And then I got that scary text message in

the middle of the night. And my phone was on—not the way I left it when we went to sleep. This afternoon, I had that creepy feeling that someone was watching me again—and I saw a red-haired girl running away from my window! When I got back to my room, my top was NOT where I left it and I found it shredded in my closet. All that stuff is VERY weird. Don't you agree?

Then things got even scarier. Leah, I got another freaky text message from that same strange number! And this time, I wanted to know who sent it, so that maybe I could stop them from sending another. But when I tried to look the number up online, my computer froze for no reason. Then my room went icy cold. I was terrified. If just one or two of these things happened, I would think it was a coincidence. Or maybe even my imagination. But all of them, together . . . I mean, how could I imagine those texts? Or my top getting ripped up? Those things are completely real, and you can come see them for yourself if you don't believe me.

I need to make this stop NOW, and I have an idea, but I'd like your help. Can you meet me at school tomorrow morning before class starts? Like, eight a.m.? You are my best friend, Leah. Please help.

<3
Abby

Abby read her e-mail to Leah twice before she took a deep breath and sent it. She didn't know how Leah would respond, but she also knew that if Leah wouldn't take her seriously, she'd have to move forward on her own.

No matter how terrifying or dangerous it would be.

CHAPTER 8

Thursday morning dawned cool and cloudy; Abby woke up earlier than usual after a long and restless night. Even with her bedroom door wide open and Chester sleeping peacefully at the foot of her bed, she had tossed and turned, alert to every little noise in the night. When she finally got out of bed just before her alarm went off, Abby stepped over to the window and saw damp mist seeping out of the woods into her backyard. She shivered as she pulled the gauzy curtains back across the window. She knew that she couldn't be too careful; there was no telling who—or what—might be out there.

Then she walked over to her computer to see if Leah had e-mailed her. By the time Abby went to bed, Leah hadn't responded, which was so unusual it made Abby even more anxious. Abby didn't know anyone who was more addicted to the Internet than Leah, so there was no possible way she hadn't received the e-mail. The only explanation for her lack of response was that Leah was ignoring her.

To Abby's relief, though, she saw that she had an e-mail waiting from Leah. It was short, but Abby didn't care.

> **To:** AbbyGirl
> **From:** Leah601
> **Subject:** Re: Sorry
> Hey Abby,
> Everything is going to be fine. I'll meet u @ the flagpole. L.

Abby got dressed and grabbed a stack of pages that she'd printed off the Internet the night before. When she went to the kitchen, she found her mom drinking coffee and reading the newspaper at the table.

"Morning, Abby," Mrs. Miller said. "How did you sleep last night? Was your room warm enough?"

"Uh, yeah," Abby said as she grabbed a box of cereal out of the cupboard. "It was fine."

"You're up early today," Mr. Miller remarked, walking into the room.

"I'm meeting Leah before school," replied Abby. "We, um, have a project to work on. That reminds me, can she come over after school today?"

"I don't see why not—as long as it's okay with her parents," Mrs. Miller said. "Dad and I are going out to dinner with the Takahashis, remember? So we won't be here. Do you mind heating up some leftovers for dinner?"

"Sure," Abby said, grateful that her parents would be out. "Leah and I will mostly be working on that project."

"Well, we'll probably be home around eight. Then we can drive Leah home," Mr. Miller said. "Speaking of rides, do you want me to drive you to school? I'm headed out for work in a few minutes."

Abby smiled at her dad as she quickly ate her cereal. "That would be great. Thanks, Dad." When she was finished, she put her bowl in the sink and said, "Okay, I'm off. See you tonight, Mom."

"Bye, Abby," Mrs. Miller replied. "Have a good day!"

Abby pulled on her coat and picked up her backpack as her mom went back to the newspaper. Standing in the cozy, cheerful kitchen, it was hard to believe that such scary things had been happening. Abby wished, briefly, that they would just stop on their own. That life would go back to normal.

But she knew that that wasn't going to happen—unless she did something about it.

During the car ride with her dad, Abby noticed how much emptier the streets and sidewalks were at this early hour. As the car neared the school, she started to feel more and more nervous about meeting up with Leah. What if Leah didn't want to help her? What if Leah laughed at her plan?

That's just a risk I have to take, Abby told herself.

The schoolyard was empty when she walked through the heavy black gate, though the lights were already on and she could see teachers arriving in the faculty parking lot. She sat on the round concrete base of the flagpole and glanced up at the cloud-covered sky; overhead, the flag flapped loudly as gusts of wind blew in from the west. Abby glanced at her watch.

Leah was late.

Abby had a sinking feeling that Leah wasn't going to show up. *Maybe she forgot*, she thought. *Or maybe she was never going to come in the first place.* She didn't know what had happened to make Leah so mad at her, but she really needed her best friend now.

As she waited, Abby's feet started tapping, then her knees started jumping, until she was suddenly too anxious to sit still for another minute. She stood up and started pacing near the flagpole, watching silently as more students arrived for the school day. *Where is Leah?* Abby wondered frantically. *Has something happened to her? What if Sara's ghost—*

Abby couldn't finish that thought.

With just five minutes left before homeroom, she had to face the truth: Leah wasn't coming. For the first time in her life, Abby actually hoped that Leah had blown her off; that would be better than the other possibilities that wouldn't stop running through her mind. She stood up and was slipping the strap of her backpack over her shoulder when she heard someone call her name.

"Abby!"

It was Leah.

"You're here!" Abby exclaimed, rushing up to Leah. "I was so afraid! I thought you—"

"I'm fine. I just overslept," Leah said, her voice full of concern. "You have to relax."

But Abby noticed that Leah wouldn't meet her eye. The girls stood there awkwardly for a moment. Then they both spoke at the same time.

"So what do you—," Leah began.

"Did I do something—," Abby said.

They exchanged a smile. "You first," Leah said.

Abby took a deep breath. "Did I do something to upset you?" she asked bluntly. "I don't know why you were mad at me last night."

Leah looked away. "Just—it's not important," she said. "I read your e-mail."

"I know," Abby said quietly. She waited for Leah to continue.

"It's not that I don't believe you," Leah said. "But here's what I *don't* believe in: ghosts. I mean, they're really creepy and spooky to think about, but they're not real, Abby. Dead is dead. And Sara is dead. That's it."

Abby was silent for a moment. Then she reached into her pocket and pulled out her cell phone. She scrolled through her most recent text messages and shoved the phone at Leah. "I *know* Sara's dead!" Abby cried. "But read this latest message. Just read it!"

Leah's blue eyes flicked back and forth as she glanced

at the screen of Abby's phone. "So you think this message is about Jake?" she asked.

"Who else would it be about?" Abby asked. "Whoever is sending those messages wants me to stay away from 'him' and Jake is the only 'him' I'm into. And the only people who know that are you, Chloe, and Nora—and you guys would never do this to me."

"You're right about that," Leah replied.

"So who could it be?" Abby continued. "And what about when my computer froze or the cold air I felt in my room? I'm telling you, after what I read last night, this has to be a ghost."

Leah sighed. "So what's your big plan? Assuming that it's Sara's ghost, which I just can't believe. I mean, have you even thought that through? I don't think ghosts have wireless plans, you know?"

"Look, don't worry about it," Abby said. If Leah really couldn't believe in the possibility of this all being Sara's ghost, there was no point in her helping. "I'll figure something out."

"No, really," Leah persisted. "I can tell you're upset, and I want to help, Abby, I really do. And I'm sorry for what I said in the IM last night. I didn't mean it at all.

I don't even know why I said it."

The bell rang. Abby looked at Leah. "Come on—we're going to be late for homeroom."

"Okay, fine," Leah gave in. "But if you change your mind, let me know."

"I will," Abby replied. "Whoa—was that a raindrop?"

"Let's go!" Leah exclaimed. As the rain started to fall, the two girls raced toward the school. By the time Abby sat down in her seat for homeroom, she was out of breath and soaked. But not even the drenching rain and the rush to homeroom were enough to make her forget for a second about the strange experiences that had been haunting her.

That evening, as it started to get dark out, Abby put her plan into motion. The website had said that the séance would work better if two or three people were involved, but Abby would just have to make do on her own. Leah just didn't understand.

In the quiet of her room, she cleared off the top of her dresser and placed a photo of Sara in the very center of it. She surrounded the photo with a circle of softly glowing lights and white rose petals. *Sara should still be alive, like me and Jake and Leah*, she thought suddenly. *She shouldn't exist only in photos and memories.*

But Abby knew that there was no way to undo the tragedy that had cut Sara's life short. So if Sara's spirit was having trouble crossing over to the other side, Abby was determined to help her.

Next, Abby draped a dark cloth over the mirror. Whatever it might reflect in the next hour, she didn't want to see it—not when she was all alone. With the lights off and the door closed, her room suddenly felt as dark and cramped as a crypt. She closed her eyes and reminded herself that this was the only option she had. There was no point in letting fear get the better of her—not when she'd been so frightened already.

Abby sat on her bed and forced herself to stare at the photo of Sara. Her green eyes gleamed in the soft light, as if they held a secret that no one else knew. After counting backward from one hundred, Abby took a deep breath and started to speak.

"Sara?" she asked softly. "Are you there? Please give me a sign if you can hear me."

Abby waited in the quiet darkness, but no sign came.

"Sara," she repeated. "I want to help you. Please, give me a sign."

This time, in the quiet, Abby started to feel a little foolish. But she pressed on.

"Give me a sign, Sara," she said, her voice growing louder. "Give me a sign."

Tap-tap-tap-tap.

Abby's whole body stiffened. "Sara?" she asked, her voice shaking. "Is that you?"

Tap-tap-tap-tap.

The sound was coming from the window.

Tap-tap-tap-tap.

Abby slowly got off her bed and walked over to the window, which was covered by the curtain. Was that a shadow on the other side of the window—or was it just her imagination? Her heart pounded wildly as she reached for the curtain with a trembling hand. She mustered all her courage, and with one swift, sudden yank, she pulled back the curtain.

On the other side of the window, a pale face stared back at her!

CHAPTER 9

"Leah!" Abby screamed as she recognized her friend. "What are you doing here?"

"Open up!" Leah yelled back, her voice muffled by the glass. "It's wet out!"

Abby unlocked the window and pushed it open. "You scared me to death!" she exclaimed. "Why were you hanging outside my window?"

"Because you wouldn't come to the door," Leah replied as she climbed into the window. "I was ringing the doorbell for, like, five minutes."

"The doorbell's broken," Abby said. "Have you ever heard of knocking?"

Leah shrugged. "What's the big deal?" she said. "I figured you'd be in your room, and here you are." Then she glanced around Abby's bedroom. "Whoa. What are you doing?"

"Nothing," Abby said quickly as she felt her face grow hot. "Just—let's go down to the basement and watch TV or something."

"Is that a *shrine?*" Leah asked incredulously as she walked over to Abby's dresser. She stared at Sara's picture, the rose petals, the gleaming lights. "Abby, did you make a *shrine* to Sara?"

"I don't want to—," Abby began.

Leah looked concerned. "This has definitely gone too far. I think you're starting to get obsessed. What are you up to here?"

"Why should I tell you?" Abby shot back. "You'll just laugh."

"No, I won't," Leah said. "I promise."

"I was trying to have a séance," Abby admitted. "I wanted to make contact with Sara to help her get to the other side."

Neither girl spoke for a moment.

"So you're really convinced that Sara's ghost has been bothering you?" Leah asked.

"It's the only explanation I can think of," Abby

replied. "I did this research on the Internet, and everything that has happened can be explained as 'paranormal phenomena.' That's the technical term, I mean. And I saw this one site that said spirits can have trouble moving on, especially if they weren't ready to die. So I . . ."

"Go on," Leah said encouragingly.

Abby sighed. "If Sara's spirit hasn't been able to move on, then I want to help her," she finished. "Go ahead. Laugh."

But Leah looked at Abby without giggling or even smiling. "That's intense," she finally said. "And you were going to hold a séance all by yourself? Weren't you scared?"

"Yeah," Abby said. "But I figured it couldn't be any worse than everything else that's been going on. I felt like I had to do something, you know?"

"So what happened?" asked Leah.

"I had just gotten started when you came along and knocked on my window!" Abby exclaimed as she started to laugh. "I was asking for a sign, and then I heard this *tap, tap, tap*."

Leah started laughing too. "No wonder you were so freaked out!" She got serious again. "You know what?" she asked. "Maybe *I'm* the sign. Maybe I'm the sign that you need two people for a séance."

Abby shook her head. "No, that's okay," she said. "Besides, séances don't work unless everybody believes."

"Come on, Abby!" Leah said. "You already got everything ready. And if Sara's spirit really is hanging around, it's a nice thing to do, helping her move on. Let's give it another try."

"Okay," Abby said slowly. "But no messing around. I don't want to do it unless we both take it seriously."

"Absolutely," Leah promised. "So, what do we do?"

Abby glanced at the printouts next to her bed. "We sit across from each other and hold hands," she told Leah. "That's to make some sort of energy connection. And then we just think and talk about Sara, and all our memories of her, to channel her spirit."

For several minutes the only sound in the room was Abby and Leah's quiet breathing. Then, with her eyes closed, Abby started speaking. "I remember Sara's first day at school," she said in a quiet voice. "Everyone wanted to meet her. Everyone wanted to be her friend."

"I remember when Sara read a poem that she wrote in English class," Leah spoke up. "It was about the ocean, and it was amazing."

A rumble of thunder sounded in the distance as

another storm approached. Rain started to fall again, harder and harder, the sound of the raindrops hitting the window like a message in a secret code. The wind moaned, low and lonely, as the shadows of quivering tree branches danced around Abby's room.

Abby knew that it was time to make contact.

"Sara, if you're there, I hope you can hear me," she began. "I know you've been trying to reach me, and I want you to know something: You will never be forgotten, Sara. Not by your family, not by your friends, not by Jake. And not by me, even though I didn't get to know you very well. I know why you're angry. It's not fair that I'm here and you're not. It's not fair that Jake is taking me to the dance and not you. We both know that if you were still alive, he would have asked you."

A jagged bolt of lightning illuminated the dark room, followed by an immediate clap of thunder that was so loud it made both girls jump. But Abby, her eyes still closed, pressed on.

"But you're not here, Sara. If you cared about Jake, and I know that you did, you would want him to go on with his life. That doesn't mean he'll forget you. But don't torture yourself by clinging to a life that's over, Sara. Move on. Move on into the spirit world. Move on."

Abby was quiet for a few moments, listening to the storm rage outside. Then, finally, she opened her eyes. To her surprise, Leah's eyes were tearing up. "Hey," she said gently. "You okay?"

"Yeah," Leah said with a loud sniff. "I just—I felt so sad for her, all of a sudden. You're right, Abby. It's *not* fair."

"No," Abby said sadly. "It isn't."

"Did you feel like Sara's spirit was here?" Leah asked. "I tried to believe, but I didn't feel anything that was, like, a ghost or anything."

Abby shrugged. "I don't know," she said. "But we did what we could."

Ping!

"That was my computer!" Abby exclaimed as she laughed nervously. "Uh, I guess the séance is over." She turned on the monitor and clicked on her e-mail. For a moment she didn't say a word.

"Anything interesting?" Leah asked as she pulled the cloth off Abby's mirror and started fixing her eye makeup.

"Leah?" Abby asked. Her voice was high and tight. "Can—can you come look at this?"

"Sure. What's up?" Leah asked. She peered over

Abby's shoulder at the computer screen. At the top of the e-mail window, the girls read:

TO	FROM	SUBJECT
AbbyGirl	sarajAmEs	READ IF YOU DARE

"Whoa. What is that?" Leah asked slowly.

"It's—it's Sara's old e-mail address," Abby stammered. "But this e-mail was just sent!"

"You'd better open it, Abby," Leah said. When Abby hesitated, Leah reached forward and clicked on the e-mail. In an instant, it filled the whole computer screen.

PRESENT FOR JAKE IN YOUR TOP DRESSER DRAWER.

"Oh, no," Abby whispered. "This séance was a terrible idea."

"Maybe not," Leah said hopefully. "I mean, maybe Sara had a message that she needed to give to Jake, and by contacting her you made that possible! Maybe now her spirit will be free to go to the other side!"

But Abby was filled with horrible dread. "I don't

think so, Leah," she said. "I have a really bad feeling about this."

"Just go see what it is," Leah encouraged her. "Just go see if there's even anything there."

Abby walked over to her dresser, where Sara's picture stared back at her, still illuminated by the glowing lights. She pulled open the top drawer and looked inside.

Socks. Her bathing suit. Old T-shirts for sleeping in.

Nothing unexpected.

Nothing unusual.

Abby was so relieved she started to laugh. "Leah, there's nothing here—," she began. But her voice trailed off when she saw it: the corner of a pale purple piece of paper. She didn't remember ever putting something like that in the drawer. She moved a pair of socks out of the way and found a carefully folded piece of paper with Jake's name on it, written in tiny, perfect letters.

"What do I do with this?" Abby asked anxiously. "Give it to Jake? What would I say? 'Hey, Jake, I found this in my sock drawer and I think it's for you?'" She picked up the paper and suddenly caught a whiff of that strange, exotic flower again. "Do you smell that?" she asked Leah abruptly.

"Smell what?" Leah asked impatiently as she grabbed the paper out of Abby's hand. "I want to read it."

"Maybe we shouldn't," Abby wondered aloud. "It could just make things worse."

But it was too late. Leah had already unfolded the paper. Abby watched her eyes move back and forth as she read whatever was written there.

"Well? What does it say?" Abby asked.

Leah crumpled the paper into a ball and threw it in the trash. "Never mind," she said firmly. "It was stupid. It was nothing."

"Forget that," Abby said as she reached into the trash. "I want to know what it said!"

"Abby, don't—," Leah began.

Abby smoothed out the wrinkled paper. She stood completely still as she stared at the note. The message on it wasn't long.

Truth time, Jake. What do you see in Abby? You can do better!

Abby inhaled sharply. She wanted to forget every word of the note, but she knew that the message was burned into her memory forever. She stared into the dresser drawer so that Leah couldn't see the tears that filled her eyes.

"I'm so sorry. I wish I hadn't read it. I wish *you* hadn't read it," Leah said miserably. "It was so mean. And so harsh. And totally not true! I never knew Sara was so mean. Abby? Abby? What's wrong? You look like you're going to pass out!"

Abby reached into the drawer, picked something up, and turned toward Leah. "There's something else in here," she said, her voice hoarse.

Abby held out her hand to Leah and uncurled her fingers.

A lock of long red hair tied together with a purple bow gleamed in her palm.

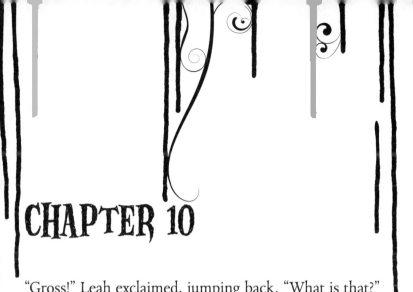

CHAPTER 10

"Gross!" Leah exclaimed, jumping back. "What is that?"

"It's hair," Abby said with a shudder. "Red hair. Leah, if you can come up with a reasonable explanation for this, I'm dying to hear it."

Leah just looked at her with wide eyes. "Abby, I don't know what to say," she replied. "You . . . haven't started collecting other people's hair, have you?"

Abby turned away. "This isn't funny," she said coldly. "Sorry if my sense of humor is failing me right now."

"No, *I'm* sorry," Leah replied as she stared at the floor. "I didn't mean for that to sound sarcastic. You need a totally supportive friend now more than ever, and I've been an epic fail in that department. This is all just very hard to believe."

"Tell me about it." Abby sighed. "It seems obvious, though, that Sara's . . . spirit has been here. She was probably here the night of my sleepover, too, when she moved my cell phone and turned it on and all that."

Leah sighed too. "Abby?"

"Yeah?"

"I . . . never mind," Leah said awkwardly. But there was something about the expression on her face that made Abby narrow her eyes and take a closer look at her friend.

"What is it?" Abby asked.

"Forget it," Leah replied.

"Leah, if you don't tell me right now—," Abby said, her temper starting to rise.

"Okay, okay, I have to confess something," Leah said as she held up her hands. "At your sleepover, after everyone went to bed, I couldn't sleep, and I was wondering if Jake had texted you back. Maybe he had told you that Max mentioned me. So I got up and I, well, borrowed your cell. Just to see if Jake texted you again."

"You went snooping around in my phone?" Abby cried.

"No! Not exactly. Well . . . kind of," Leah admitted.

"I know, I know. I didn't have any right to do that. But I was really curious, and honestly, I didn't even know if you would tell me if he *did* text you again. You're so secretive sometimes."

"I can't believe you did that," Abby said. "It was *none* of your business. No wonder I'm secretive when you're always invading my privacy."

"Ouch," Leah said. "That was mean."

"But true," Abby said. "So did you send me that scary text message, too?"

"No!" exclaimed Leah, looking genuinely hurt. "Abby, I would never do something like that."

"So all this time when I was wondering how my phone got moved, how it seemed to turn on by itself—that was you?" Abby asked, shaking her head. "And you just let me keep wondering about it instead of confessing?"

"I was embarrassed," Leah said. "But do you understand now why I kept telling you that there had to be a reasonable explanation? Because those things *seemed* really creepy, but there was a perfectly rational explanation for them."

"Except for the scary message—I mean *messages*,"

Abby pointed out. "And the ripped-up top, and this hair in my drawer, and—"

"I get it," Leah cut her off. "And I can't explain that stuff, Abby. I wish I could, but I can't."

There was a pause as Abby tried to think of something to say. Suddenly Leah continued. "You don't understand, Abby. It's so *easy* for you."

"Excuse me?" Abby asked. "Easy for me that I have some crazy *ghost* stalking me?"

"Not that," Leah said, shaking her head. "You can text Jake. You can talk to him like it's no big deal. And then, surprise, he asks you to the dance. But I've had a crush on Max *forever* and he barely knows that I even exist."

"Because you never talk to him!" Abby exclaimed.

"Because I'm scared I'll say something stupid!" Leah retorted.

Abby sighed. "Do you want me to talk to Jake? Find out who Max likes?"

"No. Maybe. I'm not sure," Leah replied. "I'll think about it. But speaking of Jake, what are you going to do?"

"Do?"

"Well . . . you know . . .," Leah said, gesturing to the photo of Sara on Abby's dresser. "Are you still going to go to the dance with him?"

For a moment Abby didn't answer as she turned away from Leah and stared at Sara's picture. Then she picked up the photo and slowly tore it in half with a loud, satisfying *riiiiipppppp*.

"You bet I am," she replied as she dropped the torn photo in the trash. "I'm not going to let some *ghost* keep me from living my life."

Leah raised her eyebrows. "Wow," she said. "Go, Abby. You're so brave."

Abby glanced at the lock of red hair and the crumpled-up note that had accompanied it. "What choice do I have?" she asked.

CHAPTER 11

By the time Saturday evening came around, though, Abby's courage began to waver. Friday and Saturday were thankfully uneventful, but Abby hadn't gotten a good night's sleep since her sleepover. She was exhausted as she got ready for the dance. She peered at herself in the mirror and frowned. "There's not enough makeup in the world to get rid of these circles," Abby said as she dabbed concealer over the dark shadows beneath her eyes.

"Don't be silly. You look beautiful!" Mrs. Miller replied as she reached for Abby's hairbrush. "Let's put your hair up a little. Just to see how it looks."

"Mom. My hair is fine," Abby said. "Leave it alone."

"Okay." Mrs. Miller sighed. "It just looks so pretty

when you clip it up. See what I mean?"

"But I want to wear it down," Abby argued, pushing away her mom's hands.

"Okay, okay! Honey, you seem so nervous," Mrs. Miller said, her voice filled with concern. "Jake is such a nice boy. Just try to relax and have fun tonight!"

If she only knew, Abby thought. "I will, Mom," she replied, hoping that her voice sounded normal. "Sorry I snapped at you. I'm a little stressed."

"You look wonderful, and you're going to have a great time," Mrs. Miller said. "I just know it!"

I hope so, Abby thought as she tried to smile at her mom.

But she wasn't so sure.

Just then there was a loud knock at the front door. "That must be Jake," Abby said as she jumped up. "I've gotta go."

From the hallway, she could hear her father's voice. "Hello, Jake. Why don't you come inside and sit down for a minute? I thought we could have a nice chat before you whisk my daughter away into the night."

A look of horror crossed Abby's face. "Mom, *no!*" she whispered. The absolute last thing Abby wanted Jake to deal with was her dad and his sense of humor—or lack thereof.

"Hurry," her mom said, patting Abby's arm. "I'll get your coat."

Abby darted into the living room. "Hi, Jake," she said with a little wave. "Well, we better get going. See you later, Dad!"

But Mr. Miller wasn't quite done. "You'll have her home by nine thirty, of course," he said to Jake, raising an eyebrow at him.

"Um, yes, absolutely," replied Jake. "My mom's picking us up at nine fifteen, so that won't be a problem."

"No, I didn't think it would be," Mr. Miller said, with a twinkle in his eye.

"Come on! Let's go!" Abby exclaimed as she grabbed the sleeve of Jake's coat and pulled him toward the front door.

"Here you go, Abby," Mrs. Miller said as she handed Abby her coat. "Have fun!"

Abby breathed a sigh of relief as she and Jake stepped outside into the twilight.

"Hey," Jake said as he flashed Abby a smile. "You look nice."

"Thanks," she said, blushing as she followed Jake out to his mom's car. "Sorry about my dad." But one thing Abby wasn't sorry about was the lock of hair and the note that were crammed in the trash can in her room—presents for Jake that he would never receive.

As she buckled her seat belt, Abby felt her cell phone buzz with a text message. She reached for it, but suddenly stopped herself. *It's not Mom or Dad*, she thought. *And if it's Leah, I'll see her in five minutes. So I'm not even going to look at this text.*

The short drive to the school passed quickly, thanks to Mrs. Chilson's friendly chatter. "Bye, kids," she called out as Abby and Jake climbed out of the car. "I'll pick you up in front, okay?"

Abby and Jake thanked her for the ride and walked around the school to the gym, where the dance was being held. As Jake held open the door for her, Abby gasped in delight. The gym had been transformed! The walls were covered with shimmering dark purple fabric; thousands of twinkling lights looped across the ceiling like constellations from another galaxy. At one end of the gym, a row of refreshment tables was decorated with garlands of white roses that perfumed the entire room.

"It's beautiful!" Abby exclaimed, her eyes shining happily. She had never imagined that the gym could be transformed into such a romantic and magical place.

The dance was already about a hundred times better than any dance she'd been to before.

But when Jake didn't respond, Abby turned to glance at him. The look of dread on his face told her that the dance was the last place in the world that he wanted to be.

"Jake?" Abby asked quietly. "Is—um—is something wrong?"

Jake shrugged and tried to smile at her. "No, no," he said. "Ready to go in?"

"Sure," Abby said, trying to sound friendly. Trying to sound normal.

Jake hesitated for just a moment, then reached for her hand. His fingers were smooth and warm as he entwined them with hers.

Abby's heart started pounding so loudly that she was sure everyone in the gym could hear it. She felt the blood rush into her cheeks and was grateful that it was too dark for anyone to notice. Because in that sweet moment, and despite everything that had happened in the past week, Abby was overcome with such happiness that it almost made her dizzy.

Inside the gym, she could see Morgan Matthews fluttering around anxiously, making sure that everything was set up perfectly. And across the room, she spotted Chloe and Nora. Her friends smiled and waved to her. Then Abby saw something that made the biggest, brightest smile stretch across her face: Max Menendez, carrying two cups of fruit punch, walking over to Leah. Abby giggled when she saw the look on her friend's face—somehow her expression was a combination of astonishment, excitement, and utter delight. Abby realized that she'd never seen Leah look so happy . . . or so pretty. *We're gonna be on the phone all night for sure*, Abby thought, thrilled that Max and Leah were finally spending time together.

But as Jake and Abby moved farther into the gym, the smile faded from Abby's face. She saw, then, what Jake had noticed the moment they had arrived: an enormous portrait of Sara hanging from the ceiling, watching all of them with her haunting green eyes. The portrait had been painted in such a lifelike style that Sara's eyes almost seemed to glow. Abby glanced at Jake's face and saw that he couldn't take his eyes off the portrait, try as he might.

Does he see what's really there? she wondered suddenly. To Abby, those green eyes seemed evil. The thin red lips were pursed in anger. She could find no trace of beauty in Sara's portrait anymore.

Maybe it was the lack of sleep.

Maybe it was the culmination of her week of fear.

But Abby knew that she couldn't do this—not here, not now, not with him.

"I'm sorry," she whispered to Jake as her hand fell out of his. "I can't."

Then Abby turned away and ran from the room.

CHAPTER 12

"Abby, wait!"

She heard Jake calling after her but she kept running, away from the gym, away from the portrait, away from the boy who was so clearly still crazy about a dead girl. With a ghost.

"Please, Abby!" Jake begged as he caught up to her in the hallway and grabbed her arm. "Give me—"

"No," Abby said, shaking her head. "You can't—"

"Try to understand," Jake interrupted her. "I knew that the money from the dance was going to her scholarship, but I didn't expect the gym to be turned into such a huge memorial to Sara, okay? The purple decorations? Her favorite color. The white roses? Her favorite flower. And that portrait . . . Living in this town, going to this school, there are reminders of her *everywhere*. I can't even take a girl I *like* to a dance without feeling like Sara's watching me."

"Because she is!" Abby exploded. Then she clapped her hands over her mouth in horror.

"What did you say?" Jake asked.

"Never mind," Abby said quickly. "I'm just going to call my mom and get out of here, okay?"

"No," Jake insisted. "I want to know what you meant by that."

Abby's resolve wavered as she looked into Jake's eyes. *He deserves to know the truth*, she thought. *But can he handle it?*

Then Abby realized that that wasn't her decision to make.

"I don't even know where to begin," she said slowly. She took a deep breath. And she told Jake everything.

Everything.

Jake listened quietly, never interrupting her, but Abby couldn't help noticing the way his eyes narrowed and his lips grew thin and sullen. Near the end of her story she realized that she had made a huge mistake.

But there was no turning back now.

"I know it sounds crazy," Abby finished. "I know it does. But there is no other explanation that I can figure out. Sara's spirit hasn't moved on. She's still in love with you, Jake, and she doesn't want anyone to take her place in your heart."

Abby held her breath as she waited for Jake's response. For a moment he looked angry. But then his anger melted away.

"Abby," he said gently, "it doesn't just sound crazy. It *is* crazy."

Abby sighed. "Okay," she said. "I'm going home now."

"Wait," Jake insisted. "I know you didn't know her well, but Sara was a really nice person. Like, genuinely nice. She would never try to scare someone or upset them in any way. I mean, you've known *me* forever. Do you think I'd go out with someone like that?"

Abby grabbed her cell phone and shoved it at Jake. "I haven't even read this text yet," she said. "But I can guess who it's from."

Abby held her breath as Jake's eyes flicked over the screen of her phone. One look at his face told her she was right. But then he shrugged as he handed the phone back to her.

"There's no proof that this message is from Sara," Jake said. "I don't even recognize the number it came from."

"But who—," Abby began.

"Don't get me wrong," Jake continued. "It's terrible that you're getting messages like this. I just don't believe that they're from Sara."

Abby looked down at the screen so Jake wouldn't see the tears in her eyes. At last, she read the message for herself.

DO YOU DARE GO TO THE DANCE WITH JAKE? HERE'S THE TRUTH: IF YOU GO TO THE DANCE WITH HIM, YOU WILL BE SO SORRY.

"I mean, whoever is sending these messages is just a bully," Jake said. "Don't give in. Come back to the dance with me, Abby. Or we could get out of here altogether— go get some pizza or something—just you and me, and forget all about what we saw in there."

As if he could sense Abby's hesitation, Jake pressed on. "Listen. I can tell you're convinced that Sara's ghost is behind those messages," he said in a rush. "So make her prove it. Write back and ask for *proof*—something that only Sara could tell you."

"Fine." Abby sighed. Her fingers fluttered across the

keypad as she typed, IS THIS REALLY SARA? PROVE IT! Then, before she could lose her nerve, she hit send.

Abby and Jake were quiet for a moment as they waited for a response. Seconds stretched into minutes until Jake suddenly laughed so loudly that Abby jumped.

"See?" he said joyfully. "It was just a prank. Whoever was sending those messages has nothing to say now! So how about it, Abby? Want to go—"

BZZZZZ!

The buzzing of Abby's phone silenced Jake and wiped the grin from his face. "Well?" he asked, with just the hint of a tremor in his voice. "What does it say?"

Abby glanced at the screen as her face filled with confusion. "I don't understand what this means," she said, shaking her head. She handed the phone to Jake so he could see for himself. "It's just numbers—a seven, a four, and a two."

The phone slipped from Jake's hands, clattering loudly on the linoleum floor. His face was like a mask, empty of all emotion except for terror.

"What is it?" Abby asked in a panic. "What's wrong?"

"It's *Sara!*" he gasped.

CHAPTER 13

"Jake?" Abby asked urgently. "Jake! What does that mean?"

But Jake just stared at her with wide, scared eyes.

"Jake!" she cried again, grabbing his arm. "Tell me what it means!"

Abby's touch seemed to snap Jake out of his daze. He opened his mouth, closed it, shook his head. "I can't—," he began. "It's not possible—"

"What's going on?" Abby begged.

Jake closed his eyes as he sighed heavily. "It was our secret," he said. His voice was halting, unsure. "Sara and I had this secret code. Every night before I went to bed, I'd send her an e-mail that said, 'XOXO 24/7.' And when I woke up in the morning, I always had an e-mail waiting from her that said, '7-4-2, OXOX, a mirror of my message.' After a while, she started texting me the number 7-4-2 during the day, after classes, on the weekends—you know, whenever. It was her way of telling me that she—that she was thinking about me. And no one in the world knew what it meant, except for the two of us. I never told anyone except for you, right now."

Abby sucked in her breath sharply. This, more than anything else that had happened, confirmed her deepest fears.

"Listen," Abby said slowly. "Don't freak out. But I have an idea."

"What is it?" asked Jake.

"You asked for proof—and you got it," Abby continued. "So let's take this to the next level."

Abby bent down to the floor and picked up her phone. She started typing a text message as Jake stared over her shoulder.

SARA, JAKE IS HERE. HE MISSES YOU. CAN HE SEE YOU?

"Abby, wait—," Jake began.

But it was too late. Abby had already pressed send.

"Why did you do that?" Jake exclaimed. "What were you thinking?"

"Jake, this has to end," Abby said. "I can't have Sara's spirit *haunting* me like this. And it doesn't matter if you stop liking me—she'll just do it to the next girl you like. And the next, and the next, and the next."

Jake shook his head. "I don't want to see her, Abby."

"She needs to move on," Abby replied. "And I think she needs your help to do it."

"But I already said good-bye to Sara—at her funeral, and every day for the last year," Jake said. "I don't want to say good-bye again."

Abby opened her mouth to reply when—

BZZZZ.

Abby read the incoming text without saying a word. Then she held the screen up to Jake so he could read it too.

I'M @ ST. RAYMOND'S CEMETERY. COME SEE ME IF YOU DARE!

Jake and Abby exchanged a glance. They were both familiar with St. Raymond's Cemetery. It was where Sara had been buried nearly a year ago.

"Come on, Jake," Abby said gently. "Let's go."

"Okay," Jake said at last. "I'll come with you. But only because it's time to put an end to this—for your sake and mine."

Abby stared at Jake's face for a moment, and the way the light had gone out of his eyes. He looked tired and angry. "What?" she asked. "You don't believe it's Sara anymore?"

"No," Jake said firmly. "And I can't believe you do either. There's no such thing as *ghosts*."

"But—," Abby began.

"Here's the other reason," Jake interrupted her. He tapped the screen of Abby's phone. "This doesn't even *sound* like Sara. She really was a sweet and wonderful person. She'd never say anything like that. . . . 'Come see me if you dare.'" Jake sighed. "If it was really Sara, she wouldn't have to dare me. She'd know that I would be there in a heartbeat."

"Right," Abby said awkwardly, feeling a flush of embarrassment for liking Jake when it was so painfully clear now that his heart belonged to someone else: a dead girl. "Let's get this over with."

Abby and Jake didn't speak as they walked down the

long hallway toward the door and stepped into the crisp, clear autumn night.

Finally Jake's voice interrupted the silence. "Abby?" he said. "I want to—I want to tell you that I'm sorry."

"For what?" Abby asked.

Jake waved his hand vaguely. "For all this," he replied. "For everything. This is not exactly what I had in mind when I asked you to the dance."

"Me neither," Abby said. And then, to her surprise, they both laughed.

"I really like you, Abby," Jake said shyly.

In the moonlight, Jake smiled at her, and Abby's heart skipped a beat, the way it always did when he looked at her. But then, slowly, his lips fell into the same sad expression that had grown so familiar to her over the last year.

This time there was something else, too: tension in his muscles and a hint of fear in his eyes as they looked past Abby.

And in that moment, she realized where they were: just steps away from the marble archway of St. Raymond's Cemetery. She shivered as the hair on the back of her neck rose, but she forced herself to look beyond the entrance, where the tombstones stood in long, silent rows, illuminated by the pale moonlight. The close-cut grass; the stone-paved paths; the carefully-carved grave markers; all of it seemed so dark and lonely on this cold, starless night. But what Abby really hated about grave-yards was the flowers. They seemed so out of place with their gaudy colors and sweet scents—especially when it was just a matter of time before they, too, died, their petals falling like tears.

Of course, worst of all were the forgotten graves, where no one bothered to leave anything.

Abby inhaled sharply. *All right. Time to go in*, she thought. She turned to Jake. "Are you ready?" she asked.

Jake nodded in reply.

Abby took a deep breath, and together they stepped into the cemetery. For a few moments, they walked in silence. Then Abby said, "Jake? I don't—I don't remember where Sara's grave is."

"It's near the back," he said. "By the border of the nature preserve."

"Oh," was all Abby said. But she thought, *Of course it is. And my house is right on the other side. How easy for Sara to—No. I won't go there. I can't.*

A cool breeze kicked up, ruffling Abby's hair and sending chills down her spine. She pulled her jacket tighter around her, but the cold creeping through her body wasn't just from the night air. As they approached the area near Sara's grave, every muscle in her body resisted, and her steps grew heavy, leaden. She wanted to run, out of the cemetery, back to the school, anywhere away from this place of deathly stillness.

But Abby knew that she had come too far to turn back now. And, of course, there was Jake. He needed her. She wouldn't let him down.

No matter how afraid she was.

She forced herself to keep walking, one step after another, remembering the feel of Jake's hand in hers back at the gym, the way her own hand had felt warmer from his touch. In this dark, quiet graveyard, that memory told her something essential: that she and Jake were alive. It seemed a silly thing to focus on, but it was exactly what Abby needed to take those terrifying steps.

Suddenly Jake stopped. He stiffened. "You—do you see that?" he asked. "Abby, please tell me you see that."

Abby's heart started pounding as she followed Jake's gaze to a gravestone that was as white as a pearl, with a single rose carved into its front. But it wasn't the stone that had captured Jake's attention; it was the pale hand resting atop it. A hand that was connected to a slender arm, one that belonged to a girl.

A girl with gleaming red hair—a bright spot of color in the dark and dreary cemetery.

CHAPTER 14

Is it Sara? Is it Sara? Abby was only vaguely aware of Jake's hand gripping hers tightly.

Abby tried to remember how to talk, how to breathe, but those ordinary abilities seemed lost to her as the girl turned to face them, standing in a beam of moonlight. And Abby knew, all of a sudden, with brilliant clarity:

It wasn't Sara.

The realization hit Jake at the same moment; Abby could tell from the way he sighed and from the way his shoulders fell, the tension in them replaced by a great relief.

The resemblance was uncanny, though. The girl had Sara's long red hair, and her creamy skin, and even her glowing green eyes. But her nose was narrower and her chin pointier; all around, the girl seemed somehow sharper and more angular.

And far more alive. That was certain.

Jake spoke first. "Who are you?" he asked, and his voice was harsh. Angry.

"My name is Samantha," she said in a clipped English accent. "Hello."

"Hello?" Jake asked. "Hello? You're going to have to do better than 'hello.' Because you have a *lot* of explaining to do."

Abby placed her hand gently on Jake's arm. Then she turned to face the stranger. "Who are you?" she asked. "I mean, really—who *are* you?"

Samantha sighed. "I'm Sara's cousin," she replied. "I live in London with my mum. But she's on special assignment for her work, traveling through Africa, so I've come to live with my aunt Stacy and uncle Steven for six weeks."

"Sara's parents?" asked Abby. Next to her, Jake nodded.

"I was so excited," Samantha said. "I'd never been to America before. I was going to go to a new school and make new friends and everything. And Mum told me that Aunt Stacy and Uncle Steven couldn't wait for me to arrive. They hadn't seen me in years and their house had been too quiet since . . ."

Samantha looked down at Sara's grave. Then she cleared her throat and continued speaking. "But at the airport I could tell everything had gone wrong already. Aunt Stacy burst into tears the moment she saw me."

"Because you look so much like Sara?" Abby guessed.

Samantha nodded in response. "I was supposed to go to school here. Your school. But by suppertime Uncle Steven told me that wouldn't be possible. He said it would upset the students too much to see me, so I'd have to be homeschooled. They didn't even think I should leave the house. Suddenly I was to be like a prisoner in their home for six weeks, with nowhere to go and nothing to do except schoolwork all by myself, and I couldn't even reach my mum to tell her how awful it was. All my dreams for my visit were ruined. And every time she saw me, Aunt Stacy started to cry. It's been horrible.

"I started spending all my time in Sara's room, with the door closed," Samantha continued. "Just to spare my poor aunt Stacy the sight of me. And I did something bad. I started reading Sara's diary. And her e-mails. I learned all about her school and her friends and her boyfriend.

130

She did all the things I might have done here if only I didn't look so much like her," she added bitterly.

"So you went through all of Sara's stuff," Jake finally spoke up. "And then what? You wanted to, like, take over her life?"

"You have to understand. I haven't seen Sara since we were, like, three years old," Samantha replied, visibly upset with herself. "So of course I was sad to hear that she died, but I didn't *know* her. I didn't even know anything about her until I started living in her room. Aunt Stacy and Uncle Steven hadn't changed a thing about it. Even Sara's e-mail account was still active. And it wasn't hard to guess her e-mail password—JAKE."

Samantha turned to Jake. "I know I never should have done it," she said. "But I read all the e-mails you sent her. You were always so sweet and funny and really lovely to her. Nothing like the boys at home. I wanted to meet you more than anything. Because I thought if you'd liked Sara, maybe you might like me as well."

Abby spoke quickly, before Jake could respond. "I don't understand. If you were stuck in Sara's room, how did you even know about me or that Jake and I were . . ."

"One day I couldn't take it any longer," Samantha

explained. "I simply *had* to get out of that house. Uncle Steven was out, and Aunt Stacy was asleep, so I pinned my hair under a cap and put on my sunglasses and snuck out! I took Sara's bike out of the garage and just rode down the street, feeling the sun, breathing the fresh air, and then I came to a bunch of shops, and I went into one—a grocery store, it was. And—you were there, Abby. You and your friend . . . the blond one . . ."

"Leah," Abby said.

"And you both seemed so happy, and I wished so much that I was going to your sleepover party that night." Samantha covered her face with her hands. "What I did next . . . I'm so embarrassed. I followed your mum's car home, Abby. I thought that maybe even if I couldn't really attend your party, I could still listen to all the fun you and your friends would have."

Abby suddenly remembered something. "Were you in the woods early in the evening?" she asked.

Samantha nodded miserably. "I heard you call out, but I couldn't answer, of course. And then once the sleepover started, I sat by the basement window. And then I overheard you talking about Jake and I ran back home. By the time I got back to Uncle Steven's house, I was so angry and so jealous. Because if Jake started to go out with you, what chance was there for me?"

"So you texted me," Abby continued for her. "In the middle of the night, from your own phone. That's why I didn't recognize the number."

"I just wanted to frighten you enough that you'd stay away from Jake," Samantha admitted. "But then I was hanging around outside the school a few days later and I saw you walking home with him and I followed you. I heard every word you said. You'd be surprised how easily you can follow someone and never be noticed. Neither of you ever even knew I was there!"

Samantha paused. "Well, that's not quite right, actually. Because I followed you all the way to your house, Abby, and later I even peeked in your window. You looked so happy, modeling that beautiful top in the mirror, and I was so angry! And then you nearly saw me. When you ran out of your room I climbed in the window, ripped your top, and put that note in your drawer. I don't know what happened to me. I've *never* done anything like that, *never*. It all got so out of hand. I'm so sorry, Abby. I'll buy you a new top. I promise."

Abby was so shocked by all of Samantha's confessions

that she couldn't think of a thing to say. Jake, though, didn't have that problem at all. He glared at Samantha.

"You're terrible," he said, and the quiet anger in his words made them sound even harsher. "You go through Sara's personal, private things, you follow people around, and you do all that terrible stuff to Abby? You break into her house and you destroy her shirt? You send those nasty, awful messages to scare her? What's *wrong* with you?"

"Jake," Abby spoke up, but he was too angry to stop now.

"If you didn't look just like Sara, I never would have believed you were related to her," he continued loudly. "You thought you could take over her life, but you were so wrong. You could never be as sweet and nice as Sara, and that was what really made her beautiful. That was the real reason why everybody liked her so much."

"Jake, stop," Abby said firmly.

But Jake's words hovered in the air even after he finished speaking, almost echoing off the gravestones around them. A single tear slipped down Samantha's face as she nodded.

"You're right," Samantha said. "It's all true, and I deserve it. I was so lonely—I can't begin to tell you how lonely I was—it's not an excuse, but it is an explanation, and I am so, so sorry. I wish I could go back in time and undo it all."

Abby thought suddenly of what it must have been like for Samantha—thousands of miles away from her home and family and friends, stuck in a dead girl's room, surrounded by what remained of the dead girl's life. It sounded like a nightmare. Abby wondered how she would have handled it. If it would have made her do things that were otherwise unthinkable.

"Hey," Abby said as Samantha self-consciously wiped away another tear. "Listen, I forgive you. Try not to— don't be upset. It's over."

"Abby—," Jake began.

But Abby turned to him and cut him off before he could say anything else. "What do you think Sara would do right now? Wouldn't she forgive Samantha, Jake?" she asked in a quiet voice, and in Jake's eyes, Abby saw that he agreed.

Abby gave Samantha a small, sincere smile. "Would you—would you like to hang out sometime?" she asked, with just a touch of hesitation. "I, um, might have a sleepover at my house next weekend. Do you want to come? You could meet some of my friends, and my mom can talk to your aunt and uncle and make sure it's okay for you to stay over. If you want."

Samantha's eyes were bright with surprise. "R-really?" she asked.

"Well, sure, why not?" Abby asked. "After all, you already know where I live."

There was a moment of silence, and suddenly Abby and Samantha laughed, just a little. Even Jake cracked a smile.

"Come on," Abby said with a last glance at Sara's grave, so silent and cold in the moonlight. "Let's get out of here."

EPILOGUE

Nearly a week later, Abby found herself back in her basement, surrounded by sleeping bags, a plate of double-chocolate brownies, and her best friends. But this time, there was a new face in the group: someone who looked a little familiar, sounded a little different, and was slowly, shyly, getting to know everyone.

Samantha.

"What do you guys think?" asked Chloe as she lugged her enormous makeup kit over to the table. "Makeover time?"

"*Only* if we're absolutely, positively *not* going outside again tonight," Leah said firmly. She was sitting on the couch scratching Eddie's belly. The cat was purring so loudly that she was having trouble hearing her friends' chatter. "I swear I heard Toby call me Octo-Girl in gym this morning."

"No, what he *said* was, 'Watch out, girl!'" Nora laughed. "Because you were totally in the way!"

"Hey, I can't make any promises we won't go outside," Chloe said, her eyes twinkling. "I mean, maybe we'll play Truth or Dare later. And *anything* can happen during Truth or Dare."

"No, no," Abby spoke up, shaking her head. "I think we've played enough Truth or Dare for a while."

"What's the matter, Abby?" Leah asked with a giggle. "Are you worried somebody's going to ask all about your big date with *Jake* tomorrow?"

Abby grinned as the rest of the girls shrieked with excitement. "Nope," she replied. "That's not a secret. I'll tell you guys whatever you want to know."

"Well, here's what I want to know," Nora said loudly. "Everything!"

"Yeah!" cried Chloe as she plunked down next to Abby. "What are you going to wear?"

Abby caught Samantha's eye and smiled. "Samantha and I went shopping yesterday after school," she began, "and I got this great top. It's pale blue, and it has a skinny black belt. I love it."

"It looks so gorgeous on you," Samantha spoke up, and the two girls exchanged a grin.

"So what are you and Jake going to do, anyway?" asked Chloe.

"We're going to the movies," Abby said. "And then I think we're going to get ice cream after. You know, at the place down the street from the movie theater."

Leah sighed. "That sounds *so* awesome."

"Want to come?" Abby asked, her eyes twinkling.

"You know I can't." Leah giggled. "Because Max and I are going out for pizza!"

"What?!" screamed Chloe and Nora at the same time, and everyone cracked up.

"He just asked me this afternoon!" Leah said excitedly. "I couldn't believe it! I couldn't even think of anything to say, so I finally just nodded!"

"What are you going to do if that happens on your *date* tomorrow?" asked Nora.

Leah suddenly got serious. "Well, I already made a list of things we could talk about," she said. "I'm not, like, going to bring it with me or anything. But hopefully writing them down will help me remember them later!"

"You'll be *fine*," Abby said. "And if you get really stuck, just text me! We could all meet up for ice cream or something, especially since Max and Jake are best friends too."

"Well, obviously makeovers for you two are a top priority," Chloe announced. "We want you guys to look really great tomorrow night." She patted the floor in front of her. "Leah, you're up."

Leah scrambled across the room and sat cross-legged in front of Chloe. She closed her eyes as Nora reached for a container of lavender eye shadow. "I think this color will look amazing next to your pretty blue eyes," Chloe said.

"Want to try those French braids again, Nora?" Abby asked. "But maybe just one this time?"

"Sure," Nora said as she grabbed a hairbrush.

"Hey, Samantha," Abby continued. "Can I do your hair?"

"Oh, of course," Samantha said quickly. She sat down in front of Abby, and as she did, Abby smelled that exotic floral scent again. Suddenly she remembered where it was from, and her eyes lit up with recognition.

"Are you wearing Sara's perfume, Samantha?" Abby asked.

The room got very quiet as everyone looked at Samantha.

She shook her head. "No, this is my perfume," she said. But then she realized something. "Oh! We gave a bottle of this perfume to Sara every year for Christmas! Did she like it?"

Abby nodded, with the hint of a smile on her face. "She loved it. She wore it all the time. Once I asked where she got it, because I wanted to buy some, but she told me that it wasn't available here."

"It's not," Samantha said. "We buy it from a small perfumery in London. They make all the fragrances there." She paused. "I could send you a bottle, if you like. When I go back home."

"That's okay," Abby replied. "I think I'll try to find my own fragrance." She started running her fingers through Samantha's long red hair, the silky tresses slipping through her hands like water. "Your hair is so beautiful. I only wish my hair was this shiny!"

"Thank you," Samantha said, and Abby could tell from her voice that Samantha was smiling.

"Where did you cut it, anyway?" asked Abby. "It's all so straight and even. You can't even tell that you cut some off."

There was a pause.

"Cut some off?" Samantha finally asked in a puzzled voice.

"Yeah, when you left that lock of hair in my dresser drawer," Abby said. "With the note?"

"I put a note in there—for Jake," Samantha said. "But that was all."

"Wait a minute," Abby said as her hands fell away from Samantha's hair. "Are you saying that you *didn't* put a lock of hair under the note? Long red hair, tied with a purple ribbon?"

"Absolutely not!" Samantha announced as she turned around to face Abby. "I'd *never* cut off my hair. I haven't had it cut since I was four years old."

Abby's eyes grew wide as she stared at Samantha. "But if you didn't leave me a lock of red hair," she said slowly, "then who *did*?"

DO NOT FEAR—
WE HAVE ANOTHER CREEPY TALE FOR YOU!

TURN THE PAGE FOR A SNEAK PEEK AT

You're invited to a

You Can't Come in Here!

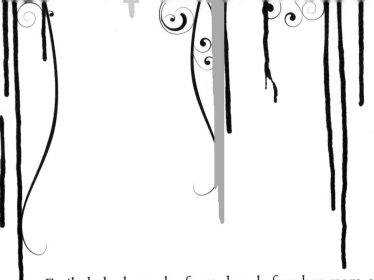

Emily bolted out the front door before her mom could say anything more. She glanced up and down the block. House after house looked pretty much the same. The soft glow of streetlights and porch lights revealed muted colored siding, sliding glass doors leading onto decks, nicely mowed lawns, landscaped gardens, and blacktop driveways.

And then there was the Strig's house.

Looking across the street Emily saw the ramshackle old place. The last few flakes of paint on the original wooden clapboard danced in the wind. The sun-bleached shutters dangled on rusty nails. Most of the windows were broken, and those that weren't were boarded up. Green moss spread across the roof. The front lawn had died long ago, and even the weeds seemed to be struggling to survive.

Emily realized that her mom was right. The place looked as if no one had lived there for years. But she knew better. A family with two kids was living there. And they liked her. They wanted to hang out with her and she liked hanging out with them. They had a lot of cool stuff in their house. And that was good enough for Emily.

She walked across the crunchy brown lawn and stepped up onto the Strig's porch. Ancient floorboards creaked as she approached the front door. Emily was about to knock when she felt a tap on her shoulder. She jumped at the touch, spun around, and found herself face-to-face with Drew Strig.

Drew was taller than Emily, and very thin. His face was pale. His jet-black hair sprang out in every direction and looked as if it hadn't had even a chance meeting with a hairbrush in years. His black T-shirt and jeans looked slightly too small for his body.

"You scared me!" Emily exclaimed and started to laugh. "I didn't hear you step onto the porch."

"Sorry about that," Drew said. "I wasn't sure you were going to make it over tonight."

"Yeah, my mom gave me a hard time," Emily explained. "You know, the usual. 'It's so late. Why are you always going over there?'"

"Maybe she doesn't like us," said a voice from above.

Looking up, Emily spotted Drew's sister, Vicky, sitting on a branch in an old gnarled tree that spread out across the front yard and overhung the tattered porch. Vicky looked very different from her brother. Her hair was pure white, but not old-lady white, more like glowing platinum. It hung down to her shoulders in perfectly straight strands extending from the part in the middle of her head. Her skin was the same color as her hair, and her thin lips had an odd purplish tint to them.

She was as skinny as her brother and almost as tall. Her black oversize shirt extended below her waist. The sleeves were so long they hid her hands. Her clothes were dirty but she didn't smell bad. She smelled kind of sweet and earthy, like the way the dirt smelled when Emily's mom churned up the garden each spring. To Emily, Vicky looked like some kind of goth-hippie hybrid. In fact, Emily thought that both Drew and Vicky dressed like rock stars. Emily, with her long, curly, reddish brown hair, sneakers instead of boots, and often sunburned face (from always forgetting to put on sunscreen before she went outside), never thought she looked as cool as these two.

"Nah," Emily responded. "It's not that she doesn't like you guys. I think she just doesn't like your house."

Vicky nodded and pushed herself off the branch. She dropped down onto the porch without making a sound and without the slightest stumble.

"Nice move," Emily said. "You should try out for the school gymnastics team."

"But I don't go to your school," Vicky said, lifting herself onto the porch railing which shifted slightly even under her light weight.

"You could probably still join the team though," said Emily. "It's a bummer you guys are homeschooled. Any chance that'll change next year?"

"Not likely," Drew answered. "Our parents would just rather have us stay home and teach us themselves."

Emily shrugged. "Your parents around tonight?" she asked, glancing up at the Strigs' house and noticing that every window was dark.

"Yeah," Drew said. "Somewhere in the house."

Emily nodded as Vicky slipped off the railing and

walked past her without making a sound. She followed, noticing that the floorboards creaked loudly beneath her own clumsy feet.

Drew pushed open the front door. It swung inward with woeful squeak. Emily followed the Strigs inside.

"Drew, Vicky? Is that you?" called out a woman's voice.

"We're upstairs," added a man's voice.

"Ah, Mom and Dad," Drew said to Emily. "Told you they were around somewhere." Then he cupped his hands around his mouth and shouted, "Yeah, it's us, Mom. Emily's here. She's gonna hang out for a while."

"Hi, Mr. and Mrs. Strig," Emily called up, as she closed the front door.

Emily followed Drew and Vicky deeper into the house. This was not the first time she had been inside, but the weird layout of the place always surprised her a bit. It was so different from her own house right across the street. Just inside the front door, there were two narrow hallways, formed by unpainted Sheetrock walls. One turned to the left. The other led to a large room that was made entirely of wood paneling. And not just the walls, but the floor and ceiling too, as if someone had found a bunch of the stuff on sale and decided to build a whole room out of it.

"Ah, the famous Strig rec room," Emily said as they stepped in.

"We like it," Vicky said, somewhat defensively.

"Hey, I like it too," Emily replied quickly. "Who wouldn't?"

The room looked as if it had been magically transported here from a college dormitory. Its main furnishings were a Ping-Pong table and a foosball table, plus a couple of ripped-up chairs and a table with an old-fashioned rotary dial phone. A line of electric guitars and amplifiers stood in a row along one wall. A stereo, complete with a record turntable, sat in one corner. Next to it stood stacks and stacks of vinyl LPs. Drew turned on the stereo and put an album on the turntable. Punk music filled the room.

"Don't your parents mind you playing music so loud?" Emily shouted as she flipped through the stack of albums.

"Nah," Drew replied. "Whose do you think these are?"

"Ready to lose?" Vicky asked, stepping up to the foosball table and grabbing the handles on one side. Emily took the other side and spun her players a few times.

"Game on," she said, dropping the ball onto the table.

Emily and Vicky slammed and twisted the game's

handles making the little plastic players they controlled kick the ball. Vicky reacted instinctively when Emily fired a shot at her goal. Her goalie blocked the shot, then she deftly passed the ball through Emily's defense and fired it into the goal.

"Ugh," Emily moaned, spinning a handle in frustration. "How are you so good at this game?"

Vicky smiled at her friend. "I've had a lot of practice. Don't worry, once you've played as much foosball as I have, you'll beat me. Another game?"

Before Emily could decide, her phone sounded with a text message. Pulling out her phone, she saw that the message was from her mother. It simply said, NINE THIRTY.

"Ah, my mother, the human alarm clock," Emily said. "Sorry, guys, I promised her I'd be home by nine thirty."

"See you tomorrow night?" Drew asked.

"Can't," Emily said. "My parents have the whole weekend planned. We're spending Saturday and Sunday at the beach. Kind of a 'summer's almost here' thing."

"Bummer," Vicky said. "But we'll see you Monday?"

"Definitely! See you later."

Emily hurried across the street and slipped into her house. Her parents were in the living room watching TV.

"I'm here!" Emily announced. "Nine thirty-two on the nose. That's what we agreed, right?"

"Cute," her mom said. "Thanks for coming home right away. Did you have fun? What did you do?"

"Played games and stuff, you know," Emily replied.

"Video games?" her mom asked.

"No, they don't have a TV, actually," Emily said. "We played foosball."

"Foosball?" her dad said. "I played that all the time in college. Great game. Maybe I could join you one time?"

"Dad!" Emily groaned.

"Just kidding," her dad said.

"All right, hon," her mother said. "Time for you to get some sleep. I'm going to wake you at seven."

Emily grimaced. Waking up early was not her thing. "Really? That early?"

"The early bird doesn't get stuck in traffic," her father reminded her.

Emily smiled as she trotted up the stairs to her room. That was one of her dad's signature corny phrases.

After brushing her teeth and changing into her pajamas, Emily flopped onto her bed, popped her earbuds in, and turned on her iPod. She imagined playing the guitar chords herself. It wasn't long before she got sleepy and took out her earbuds.

A-hooooo! Ow-ow-w! came a loud gut-piercing howl. Emily felt the blood freeze in her veins, then remembered the DVD she had been watching. *Dad must have turned on that movie. Jeez, he scared me half to—*

A-HOOOOO! OW-OW-W!

This time the howl was louder, and Emily knew instantly that it wasn't coming from the basement. The bone-chilling shriek was coming from outside.

She dashed across her room, stumbling over a stack of books she had left on the floor. Catching herself on the windowsill, she peered out the window. There, on the Strigs' brown front lawn, a huge wolf loped toward the house. The wolf's back legs were long and slender, its chest round and muscular. Matted gray fur extended down its powerful front legs in mud-stained clumps.

But it was when Emily caught sight of its jaws that her heart rose into her throat. Was that blood on the animal's snout? The wolf opened its mouth wide and howled again, revealing long white fangs flecked with specks of red.

Porch lights all up and down the block blazed to life. Seeming to notice this, the wolf glanced over its shoulder, then quickly turned back toward the Strigs' front door. Crouching low, as if it were stalking prey, the wolf slowly climbed the stairs onto the front porch.

"Drew and Vicky," Emily muttered in horror. "It's gonna hurt Drew and Vicky!"

She turned and dashed from her room. Practically flying down the stairs, she exploded out the front door. Running down the street, she felt her heart pound as she watched the wolf lunge toward the door.

"Get away from there!" Emily shouted.

At the sound of her voice, the wolf turned and stared right at her, baring its razorlike teeth and growling. Then the snarling beast turned back, pushed the door open with its snout, and walked right into the house.

"No!" Emily cried, running faster now. Reaching the porch, she took the stairs two at a time then stopped short at the front door. She pushed the door open slowly, straining to see inside without actually sticking her head through the doorway. Pushing back against the terror shooting through her body, and shoving aside all thoughts of her own safety, Emily burst into the Strigs' house.

WANT MORE CREEPINESS?

Then you're in luck, because P. J. Night has some more scares for you and your friends!

MIRROR MESSAGE

Sara James has a message from beyond the grave. Do you want to know what it is? Hold this page up to a mirror. Then have a friend read it in the mirror to find out what Sara has to say!

I AM STILL IN LOVE WITH JAKE. HE NEEDS TO KNOW. WILL YOU HELP ME?

YOU'RE INVITED TO . . .
CREATE YOUR OWN SCARY STORY!

Do you want to turn your sleepover into a creepover? Telling a spooky story is a great way to set the mood. P. J. Night has written a few sentences to get you started. Fill in the rest of the story on the lines provided and have fun scaring your friends.

You can also collaborate with your friends on this story by taking turns. Have everyone at your sleepover sit in a circle. Pick one person to start. She will add a sentence or two to the story, cover what she wrote with a piece of paper, leaving only the last word or phrase visible, and then pass the story to the next girl. Once everyone has taken a turn, read the scary story you created together aloud!

It was a dark and stormy night. The rain was tap, tap, tapping against my window and the trees were groaning in the wind. Everyone in the house was sleeping peacefully . . . except for me. There was a loud clap of thunder and then I heard something in the kitchen. It sounded like glass clinking and the floor creaking. *What could it be?* I wondered. I threw off my covers and crept out to the kitchen. I flicked on the light and saw . . .

_____

_____

_____

_____

_____

_____

_____

_____

_____

_____

_____

_____

_____

_____

_____

_____

THE END

A lifelong night owl, **P. J. NIGHT** often works furiously into the wee hours of the morning, writing down spooky tales and dreaming up new stories of the supernatural and otherworldly. Although P. J.'s whereabouts are unknown at this time, we suspect the author lives in a drafty, old mansion where the floorboards creak when no one is there and the flickering candlelight creates shadows that creep along the walls. We truly wish we could tell you more, but we've been sworn to keep P. J.'s identity a secret . . . and it's a secret we will take to our graves!